# WALK OUT

## Mike Foster

Pen Press

First published in Great Britain

All paper used in the printing of this book has been made from wood grown in managed, sustainable forests.

ISBN13: 978-1-78003-513-0

Printed and bound in the UK
Pen Press is an imprint of
Indepenpress Publishing Limited
25 Eastern Place
Brighton
BN2 1GJ

A catalogue record of this book is available from the British Library

Cover design by Jacqueline Abromeit

# WALK OUT

To Jim

with all best wishes

mike

# PREFACE

Resting hard against high cliffs as though washed up by giant waves of the Saharan sea of sand that extends westwards to the far distant Aïr Mountains, Bilma has for the past ten days found itself entrapped by the very air it breathes. So stifling is this unseasonal front of warm air that from the castellated walls of Fort Dromard – its orange, white and green Republique du Niger tricolour hanging like a dishcloth on a hook – one can hear the echoing roars of camel caravans at the nearby salines of Kalala. An air so still, so debilitating, local Kanouri and Toubou residents have ceased expending precious energies on games of date and camel dung chess in the soft sands of main street. And the mongrel packs have become noticeable by their lassitude; fights over crusts of bread abandoned they lie in deep shade flicking persistant flies with their ears and tails, attentive always to the other scavengers who share an uneasy day to day existence in this remote and dusty outpost, a gaggle of Egyptian Vultures. Bilma, an oasis in a bottle corked airtight by the Kaouar Falaise.

Through this benign calm and desperate with thirst a solitary bull Addax ventures ever-closer to the edge of the sands. Descending the final slope it again sniffs the air before entering a gulley – the same narrow defile where the previous winter his small herd had been caught in the crossfire of an army patrol that had driven south from the fort in quest of entertainment. Nervously, the antelope tugs at a tuft of

1

yellow grass, one eye on the rocks above, its long spiralled horns held parallel to a once broad back. After weeks of traversing the Grand Erg, splayed hoofs cautiously tread the unfamiliarly hard earth. Raising nostrils to a brief flow of cool air it soon comes upon a clump of tamarisk. A secondary gust rustles the leaves from which vital sustenance is drawn, before the lone Addax turns to re-enter a maze of dunes that are its permanent refuge.

In Niger's neighbouring country of Chad it is a reputed hotbed of scorpions and snakes – a small corner of Tibesti where an extraordinary cul-de-sac of towering ramparts has led these vortex-creating pillars to become known as 'Birthplace of Hell'. The cauldron of rock from which fresh prevailing north-easterlies, once clear of the mountains, swiftly gain momentum – on this day and towards nightfall bringing to the people of Bilma an initially light breeze and the cheering sound of rattling palm fronds. In less time that it takes to brew a pot of chai the sandstorm unleashess its full fury along a broad front, sweeping over the escarpment and down into the oases of Kaouar with the speed and roar of an express train. Against such unrelenting force the glass-clear bubble of motionless air is in an instant shattered into countless fragments. And come next morning the *vent de sable*, now more easterly, sees Fort Dromard's radio operator bellowing louder still into his microphone, barely able to make himself heard above a howling wind and the repetitive slamming of a wooden shutter. The response that crackles around the dust-choked room is a message from the far side of the moon, not Dirkou Fort just twenty miles to the north.

Already blown off its migratory route from northern Europe to the moist savannas of the West African coast, a Honey Buzzard attempting to seek shelter in a palm grove is suddenly lifted high into the sky where the sun is but a faint glow. Exhausted, its broad wings and fanned tail powerless in so fierce a tempest, the bird of prey is carried westwards, pitching and rolling, half-blinded by grit and dust, out over open desert. Out over – indiscernible in the Dijon mustard-coloured maelstrom five hundred feet below – a lone Addax, a Toubou and wife battling their way in a biting cross-wind from Zoo Baba to Seguedine with four camels, then a large *azalai* laden with bollards of salt that has chosen to set out on the gruelling seventeen days crossing to Agadez in sub-zero visibility. Out over the Grand Erg de Bilma, believed to have once been the northern-most shores of a once extensive Lake Mega-Chad, and on across the Ténéré.

The Ténéré Desert, a 120,000 square mile area of southern Sahara extending from the Kaouar to the Aïr Mountains and from the Tassili du Hoggar to the Termit Massif – where one hundred and more million years back in time dinosaurs roamed enormous areas of tropical forest, where eight thousand years ago Neolithic Man hunted the numerous species of wild animal then to be found in abundance along the banks of the Oued Tafassasset. A region made an ocean of sand through basaltic upheaval, water erosion and storm-force winds beyond estimation, where in the Nineteenth century intrepid adventurers began to explore this inhospitable land whilst ruthless slave-traders herded columns of black Africans from Nguigmi to Tripoli. French colonization of their West and Equatorial territories in the 'Scramble for Africa' were accompanied by a healthy respect for newly-won tracts of Sahara Desert. With forays south from Fort Charlet (Djanet) in Algeria camel corps patrols and motorised expeditions gradually mapped their progress in rather familiar style: Monts Gautier, Erg Bréard, Fort Pacot (Chirfa), Erg Brusset, Rocher Toubeau.

Niger's successive ruling parties have seen this 'uninhabited wasteland' become the focal point of many an interest and desire: an open museum with ever-shifting wind and sand patterns revealing exhibits ranging from flint artefacts to petrified wood to dinosaur bones, whilst Aïr Mountains and Djado Plateau rock art displays quite superb paintings and engravings of elephant, rhino and giraffe: a wildlife conservation area where efforts are being made to protect rapidly declining herds of highly endangered Addax Antelope and Scimitar-horned Oryx: a still not fully explored corner of the Sahara that routinely attracts semi-scientific and tour group expeditions: a mix of test site and playground for motorcycle, car and truck rallies.

Yet in every sense there remains true desert to which man is forever drawn, *Guide* and *Madugu* alike setting out on their journeys of respect and endeavour, whilst there commences an undertaking in quest of higher fulfilment still.

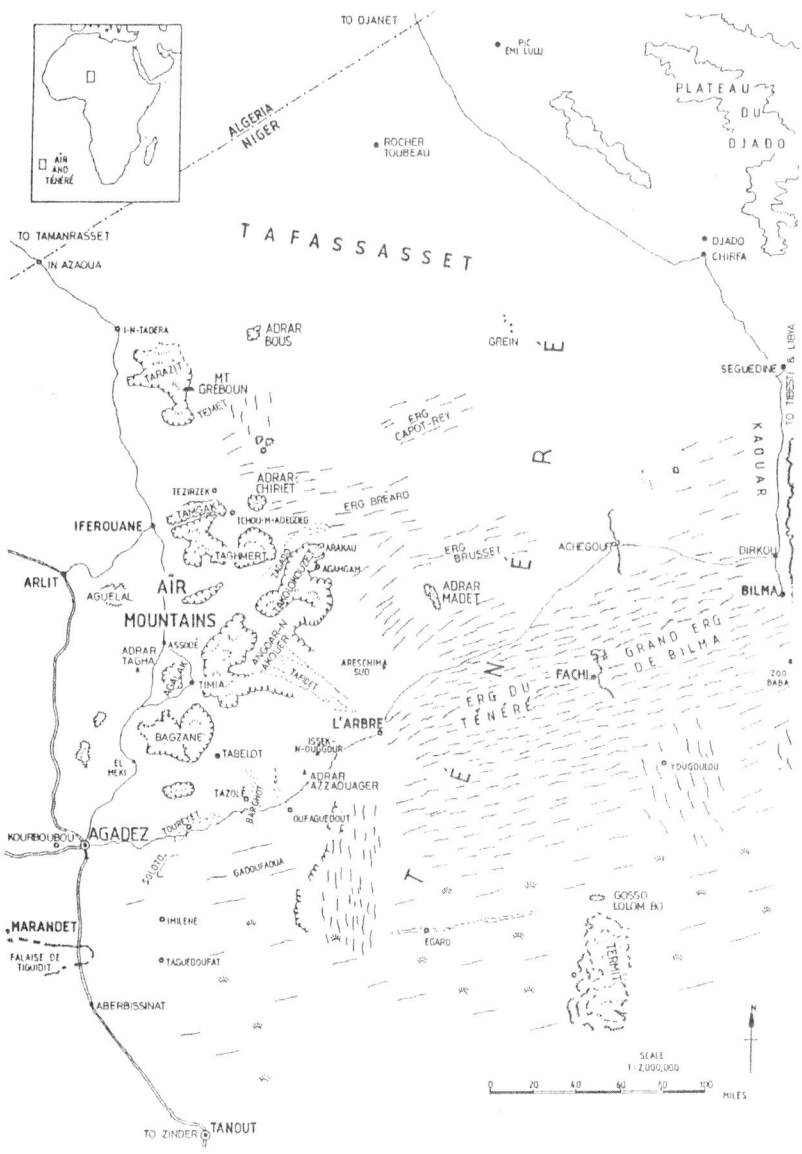

TO DJANET

PIC
EMI LULU

PLATEAU
DU
DJADO

ALGERIA
NIGER

ROCHER
TOUBEAU

TO TAMANRASSET

IN AZAOUA

T A F A S S A S S E T

DJADO
CHIRFA

I-N-TADERA

ADRAR
BOUS

GREIN

SEGUEDINE

TARAZIT

MT
GREBOUN

TEMET

ERG
CAPOT-REY

E    R

K A O U A R

TEZIRZEK

ADRAR
CHIRIET

ERG BREARD

TAMGAK

TCHOU-N-ADEDROG

ARAKAO

ERG
BRUSSET

ACHEGOUR

DIRKOU

IFEROUANE

TAGHMERT

AGAMGAM

ARLIT

AIR
MOUNTAINS

AGUELAL

ADRAR
MADET

N

GRAND ERG
DE BILMA

BILMA

ADRAR
TAGHA

ASSODE

TIMIA

ARESCHIMA
SUD

FACHI

ERG DU
TÉNÉRÉ

ZOO
BABA

BAGZANE

TABELOT

L'ARBRE

ISSEK-
N-OUGDOUR

EL
MEKI

TAZOLE

ADRAR
AZZAOUAGER

YOUGOULOU

KOURBOUBOU

AGADEZ

OUFAQUEDOUT

SOLOCO

GADOUFAOUA

GOSSO
LOLOM BO

MARANDET

IMILENE

EGARO

TERMIT

FALAISE DE
TIGUIDIT

TAGUEDOUFAT

ABERBISSINAT

N

SCALE
1:2,000,000

0    20    40    60    80    100

MILES

TO ZINDER    TANOUT

TO TIBESTI & LIBYA

5

# ONE

To a departure lounge I am no stranger... more specifically those encountered in the mish-mash of domestic airfields found around these parts, but this has to be a first... the front seats of a Land Rover. My very own long-wheelbase Land Rover this time round and not some aid agency's clapped-out Toyota. What's this, no Duty Frees here in dense scrub half a mile beyond the perimeter fence , no passport and baggage checks during my clandestine back-streets under cover of darkness exit? Surprise, surprise. Anyway, come dawn and having given the police checkpoint on the outskirts of town a suitably wide berth I will have made good my escape.

Edmund Lanby's the name – until enforced early retirement, regional supervisor with the now defunct Hydrological Services and Installations limited. Ed to most, if I'm lucky and Eddie to those for whom I have considerable respect. The likes of Hamouri here in Agadez for example, along with a former guide and interpreter who I'm hopeful of tracking down. Great shame, though, that compared to when I was last in Niger a few years ago the country is now visibly being torn apart by tribal jealousies. As if there weren't enough problems – drought-ridden still and together with neighbouring Mali one of the poorest countries in the Sahel. Everyone praying for rain, as I am that this New Year sees a break in the clouds of a few personal differences of my own. For Hamouri, his family and many others like them, Ninety-Two has begun with rather different uncertainties to mine; fear, no less, in the wake of renewed Tuareg demands for broader control of their day-to-day lives. Across this continent I've most times found local uprisings to be short-lived episodes… not always free from bloodshed, agreed, yet this latest resurgence looks to be on-going with the likelihood of further brutal crackdowns by the Hausas who are by far the largest of the various ethnic groups. This is what you find.

Earth-trembling roars rattle the jerrycans in their side-brackets as a cargo plane commences its pre-dawn take-off. I watch the aircraft's strobe lights complete a climbing turn across a sky blanketed in cloud before setting course for wherever, and now with difficulty extricate myself from this rather grubby sleeping bag to water the nearest thorn bush. Just visible between trees are the lights of a market township I regrettably find myself having to secretly depart. Absolute silence again… not even the child-like cry of a jackal scavenging through some rubbish tip. Zero three-ten, far too early for a *muezzin's* first rousing of the faithful. For mid-winter it is surprisingly warm. No woollen hat or anorak collar clasped around the lug-holes. Could have done without all this ducking and diving, have to say… hadn't envisaged such a devious end-game when setting out from London four weeks back. On the drive southwards from Morocco, hassle had been anticipated regarding the Spanish Sahara/Polisario issues, but a convoy system ensured a safe traverse through Mauritania to Dakar. Then eastwards across Mali and in the aftermath of last year's coup I encountered nothing but shining smiles and cheery waves. Only after entering Niger has it all kicked off.

As I slide back behind the wheel a gusting wind plays three-note sequences in the rookrack's fluted welding holes: 'Ag – a – dez… El – ea – nor… Ag – a – dez… El – ea – nor… No

– it would have been far better if I'd been able to share that trip out from UK. Africa is a continent with which Eleanor is unfamiliar, and remains so, more's the pity. At first the idea was received with great enthusiasm, that together we'd drive this Land Rover out to a few old stamping grounds of mine, make contact with Hamouri, spend time here, motor up in to the Aïr and visit Arambey who I imagined to have now retired to his village of Iferouane. Both widowed Elle and I, no children by either side, four and a half years shared and our close to agreeing that two can live as cheaply as one, preparations going well, when overnight with Eleanor still two years the right side of sixty and my having qualified for my bus pass there's this age-gap thing. Our first serious disagreement. 'See more of our own country... Devon and Cornwall...' A woman changing her mind I am no stranger to either. Prerogative and all that, but an irregular heart beat scare had brought home to me the realization that I couldn't postpone for a further year or more what by now was acrimoniously being labelled an escape from reality back to the memory lane of foreign lands.

On arrival here, just over a week ago, I found the Hotel de l'Aïr to be under the management of an Ivory Coast shiny-suit type sporting patent leather shoes that were collecting more dust than they ever did in Abidjan. Most gratifying to see that Amadou still ran the bar; before I'd half walked through the door after the final run-in from Assaouas he'd levered the cap off a large, cold and very welcome bottle of Flag. Disappointingly he was unforthcoming regards Pierre and Monique who, having so successfully run the hotel for many years, apparently one day packed their bags and flew back to Paris. I have a pretty fair idea why.

Next morning, after breakfasting on *deux ouefs au plat* and a gallon of black coffee, I stepped out into blinding sunlight.

And back in time. 'Oui M'sieur... donnez-moi l'argent... donnez-moi stilo...' Different faces, familiar gang, swarming around like flies as I dodged mopeds to check that nothing had been tampered with overnight. I'd parked my Series Three diesel station wagon where the Agency's four-by-fours had once stood after many a rickety drive down from Assodé or Timia. A quick check underneath confirmed that on the final leg and within sight of town, practically, one enormous pothole had taken toll of a rear spring main leaf. The howling sandstorm between Léré and Niafounké in Mali which pitted the windscreen and removed sections of limestone paint from the front wings, now seemed a necessary right of passage. The persistent, irritating posse of ragged shorts and faded T-shirts, some balancing trays of cigarettes and chewing gum on their heads, decided to tag along as I walked down side alleys to *le Commissariat*. There, documents were checked and my passport stamped. Then filed away in a drawer. Only his chief, I was told, could authorize a drive up to Iferouane. Come back at three o'clock.

My reappearance on the flight of concrete steps brought sheepishly grinning kids from out of the shadows, and back on the trail of this newly arrived greybeard in his for old times sake bush shirt and hat who may well have some spare CFA in the pockets of his strides khaki. The famous mud and exposed wooden cross-beams minaret is looking as iconic as ever, the continuously circling Pied Crows again reminding me of those seats at the end of long chains fairground rides my younger brother Harold and I used to take as kids in Dover. That was before Father's employment as a chartered accountant found the family re-locating to North London shortly before war broke out. Now it's rest in peace Mum and Dad, and Harry too. Big C. Heavy smoker.

During my absence of seven years, upon completion of the firm's final contract, Agadez's lively *Grand Marché* has grown enormously, but with correspondingly more of the same… kebab fires, lines of whirring sewing machines, bales of tie-dyed cloth, fly-blown camel meat stalls, drummers kicking up spirals of red dust. Whenever I looked around the gang buried faces in hands to conceal spontaneous laughter, then as I greeted an old friend they quickly dispersed in search of another potential source of *cadeaux*. For I've met up again with Hamouri, the quiet and unassuming silversmith cum Hydro Services middleman throughout all those confrontations with bureaucracy, and link with Arambey during HSI's three one-year well-sinking projects in and around the Aïr Mountains. Yet it is he who recognises me first, his gaunt un-veiled face, greyish pallor and rather sunken eyes are not features of *le forgeron par excellence* I once knew. His robes hang from narrow shoulders like some museum drape. Another attack of influenza… *la grippe* it's called here… but I'm certain he remains as tough as an old goat and demonstrates as much by cheerfully producing from his pockets some very fine pieces; one particular Agadez Cross genuinely wafer thin and worn away at the top by a succession of cords that for decades adorned the neck of a woman living all her life in some remote settlement in the mountains.

Hamouri and I arranged a rendezvous for the following day and I made my way back to the hotel, pestered all the way by this insanely grinning Peulh in a conical hat still plying his trade as purveyor of rather dodgy Tuareg swords. A cast-aside Niamey newspaper in reception reported fresh outbreaks of fighting between the army of Chad's President Deby and deposed Habre's rebels: to protect its citizens France had sent in Jaguar fighter bombers and a further four hundred and fifty troops. Reports of ballot-rigging in Algeria. I was again unsuccessful in putting a call through to Eleanor, our last having spoken during my Niamey stop-over.

Amadou quickly dug a beer out of the fridge, handed me the lunchtime menu and disappeared back into the kitchen. A perfunctory assessment of spirits and liqueurs running the base length of the bar's enormous mirror suggested the shelf's grimiest bottles to have remained untouched since the country celebrated its independence from France thirty-two years ago. The framed photograph of a highly decorated army officer I took to be the incumbent Ali Saibou. Ha!, talking of names… during unforgettable lights-dimmed sessions following our initial getting-together, Eleanor used to lovingly call me Mitch, on account of my middle name being Mitchell and her seeing a resemblance to a screen actor favourite of hers. Squaring my shoulders and with a wry smile I raised a glass to that mirror behind the bar in acknowledgment of a Robert Mitchum look-alike I may have once been, but most certainly was not now. How memory lane is that?

Then I did a double-take, for at the far end of the dimly-lit bar a tattered form sat slumped against the wall. Can't tell you how many such sights I've seen over the years. Ghardaïa in Algeria, for instance: sub-contract work for Sonatrach, the oil rig ex-pats' watering hole named l'Atlantide, locals swathed in their heavy *djelabas* knocking back bottles of '33' beer like there was no tomorrow. Or that afternoon even. Once saw two guys curled up in a dusty back-street waiting with empty bottles outside a store that, unusually, happened to sell wine… at the rear of a hospital too. My first experiences of such scenes in a Muslim country. All the more depressing for that.

Well fortified by a leisurely lunch I sauntered back to the police station, to at the appointed hour be taken through to an office at the end of a long corridor. Sunk deep in a swivel chair, cigarette wedged between two fingers, the lapels of his dark blue suit flecked with ash, plump Inspector Maïga bade me take a seat. The large wooden desk separating us was devoid of paperwork... ashtray, lighter, telephone, that was all. His Hausa initiation cheek scars betrayed just the hint of a smile as I politely raised a hand to the proffered packet of Rothmans. Our conversation was brief and to the point, along the lines of 'It is regrettable, Monsieur Lanby', flicking through my passport, 'but you are not permitted to travel any further. Back to Niamey, or even down to Zinder if you wish, but the mountains have now been declared a prohibited area. Blame it on the MATN.' Silently wondering 'who the hell are they', my attention drawn to the increasingly familiar photograph of a highly decorated army officer, I replied that I'd only ever been aware of the FLAA.

'Ah, yes, *Front de Liberation de l'Aïr et de l'Azzaouad* – it was they who recently clashed with our security forces near Filingue. Perhaps you...'

I confirmed that between the capital and Tahoua there'd been many roadblocks.

'Okay, *Movement d'Action des Tuaregs Nigerienne* are another collection of brigands – it is they who have been ambushing Arlit's military personnel using vehicles hi-jacked from foreign travellers south of our frontier with Algeria. I am informed that you took a rather different route for your return to this country. A very long drive, just to visit a friend in Iferouane.'

My low-key replies began to annoy as I recounted HSI's well-drilling and irrigation projects throughout the Aïr, adding that together with my former guide and translator I'd hoped we might make another camel trek up around Adrar Greboun. The mention of Arambey's name resulted in a leaning forwards, hands folded across the desk.

'I know very well your Tuareg guide, as I also know that one of his sons, Idrissa, is now active with the FLAA. It is my enormous responsibility to protect those visitors who come to this region of Niger, therefore I am unable to issue you with a *laissez-passer* to Iferouane. It will not concern you, but the authorities have also found it necessary to declare the track out to the Ténéré strictly *interdit* – camel caravans excepted, naturally, for murderous rebels are understood to be smuggling in weapons from Libya.' Denying me the opportunity to question his decision Maïga swiftly rose to his feet, handed me back my passport and wished me a trouble-free return to my country with the words 'You must realise, Monsieur, that this time you are only a tourist.'

Later that afternoon and to my utter astonishment I was successful in making not one but two phone calls. Firstly Elle, who sounded distant in both senses of the word and rejected my idea that she flew out to Agadez; that together we drove back through Mali, Mauritania and Morocco... was still angry that I had not even waited until after Christmas before, quote, 'walking out' on her.

'El –ea – nor'... 'Ag – a – dez'... right on cue another strong gust sweeps across the airfield and through the roofrack, playing its mournful dirge. Still another hour or two before the first hint of dawn.

The second call was to *la Gendarmerie* in Iferouane , my tried and tested method, way back, whenever needing to convey advanced details to my semi-nomadic coordinator. Was told that after his return from Greboun, seven or eight days ago, Arambey had set off eastwards for Tamgak to, quote, '*parler avec le désert*'. By assuming my letter had simply failed to reach him, I then realised that it was short-term memory loss, again, in that it was early each January when he used to take leave and ride off out to some solitary mountain in the Ténéré.... pay respects at his father's grave... his annual pilgrimage to Adrar Madet.

After dinner that evening I rolled my pen across the room's small writing table with the exaggerated gesture of someone risking his worldly possessions in one final throw of the dice... hitting the bottle square on.

A hangover later there I was sat on the bed, maps everywhere, deciphering scrawled arguments against taking Maïga's proclamation of unauthorised routes as gospel and lamely doing a one-eighty back the way I'd come, Eleanor's rebukes ringing in my ears. For never, I came to the conclusion, would such an opportunity present itself again. Never again would I feel physically and mentally capable of taking on the challenge of traversing a broad expanse of desert as an alternative route back home. Single-handed.

I had a good track record through past Saharan experiences, and plenty of dosh in my pocket – and above all, this fully equipped four wheel drive motor of mine in which to attempt a crossing of the now forbidden Ténéré. 'Why not?' my notes read... 'for we none of us know how long we've got.' Ever since a kid there'd existed this inherent fear of small boats that venture out of harbours... Dover harbour specifically... yet over the years, paradoxically, I've read from cover to cover the accounts of solo yachtsmen such as Francis Chichester and Chay Blythe. And the winner of the Sunday Times' Golden Globe race in '68, Robin Knox-Johnston, who competed against John Ridgeway, Bill King, Donald Crowhurst, Nigel Tetley... and most outstandingly Bernard Moitessier whose epic voyage eventually took him one and a half times around the World in his ketch 'Joshua'. Non-stop, would you believe, and the catalyst for my plan to now drive out on to the Ténéré, attempt to rendezvous with Arambey at Adrar Madet, then continue on up to Djanet in Algeria. Overall distance six hundred and fifty miles. A short letter to Eleanor has intimated that I will not be returning to UK yet-awhile.

These hours of darkness spent hiding in dense scrub are certainly a test of one's convictions, especially this raising of two fingers to the authorities. When running HSI's ops in Algeria they called me 'Two Trucks', amongst other things, having a reputation for firing anyone found going way off track in a single motor. Two vehicles minimum was my directive after some idiots went charging off on a boozed-up jolly, only for the Toyota to finish up on its side, steering mechanism mangled by one very large rock. No-one hurt, luckily, but gasping for water when finally located and rescued. Back then I'd have instantly dismissed any employee found planning to drive solo out into untracked desert. Ha!… just who is this new fellah?

The first seventy miles to Kouffaouane will be familiar… have even got some old route notes with me. Am confident that with the wide range of spares aboard I'll be okay. Should the motor decide to call it a day I'll attempt to leg it… not as books suggest just sit tight and await help. No signal flares, no radio communication either of course. On entering a prohibited area it will become my calculated and wholly accepted risk. Right now I feel there's not a lot to lose. Fair amount to gain, possibly.

Hamouri was as supportive as ever: 'Tinna, the children and I are so sorry that you will be leaving us soon, Eddie, but your journeys always were very successful and this will be no different', he'd said when given an outline of my covert plans to go in search of Arambey then continue on up to

Djanet. As a protection should he be questioned after I'd left I purposely added that I will have last been seen aiming for the road down to Zinder. Maps of the Ténéré I had none, save the indispensible sixty three miles to the inch Michelin 153. Here, he would prove as invaluable a friend as back in HSI days by obtaining, for no more than a few thousand CFA, a set of large scale charts someone had once liberated from a Paris – Dakar team. This year, he updated me, events in Algeria had resulted in that event becoming a Paris – Libya – military escort through Chad – on down to Cape Town race, creating enormous disappointment in Agadez where over many years *Le Rallye* has become a fixture in the calendar. In addition, Hamouri presented me with a sheaf of travel guidelines, in English, which he had found amongst a late relative's possessions. It dates back to the late sixties/early seventies when this Mohammedou was apparently involved with the numerous tour groups that visited this region in those days... much the same as Hamouri himself later became Mr Fixit for Hydro Services. Info compiled by a tour organizer, by the looks, but the first few pages are missing and children have scribbled their *stilos* over many of the others. From it I have learned that back then the Hotel de l'Aïr was run by a Gaston Joyce and his local wife Maria, who set up Joyce's Garden camp site after they'd been kicked out of the hotel. Touch of the *déjà vus,* managers Piere and Monique having recently flown back to France under some sort of cloud.

During my remaining days in town there ensued a game of cat and mouse after Tafou Diara decided to put in an appearance. The incorrigible Typhoo. No surprise that he's diversified from local agent for dull old flumes and water level recorders into a potential Mr Big in portable telephones. But still welcomes any hydrological work that might come his way. Following HSI's demise with redundancies across the board, was I perhaps here on associate business? Running my own company now? No, Typhoo, simply *en vacance* this time round. There was palpable grief that my visit would not result in lucrative contracts. Am pretty sure that we'd no sooner parted than he will have called someone to check if any new tenders had been issued… was Lanby now working freelance? Maybe my suspicious mind, but it seemed no coincidence that a dark maroon Peugeot would appear in my wing mirrors on the couple of occasions I paid visits to Moktar's garage.

The great Moktar – he who used to service the Toyotas. He grabbed a couple of Cokes out of the fridge , roaring with laughter as I drove into his compound, this time with my own wheels. Keita the semi-blind welder from Bamako was there as ever, working wonders with cracked exhaust manifolds and silencers. The two ancient Berliet trucks still stood on blocks, surrounded by broken springs and rusty axles half buried in sand. Moktar was certain he could lay his hands on an additional spare wheel for myLand Rover, plus inner tubes and a few jerrycans. Not privy to my plans whilst sensing a lengthy journey of sorts, he very generously gifted me a small aircraft compass… no questions asked, but quite likely a souvenir from some abandoned Dakar Rally support plane.

One afternoon and shaking off the Peugeot gumshoe I nudged my vehicle through noisy, dusty streets crowded with what could have been taken as actors turning up on the set of some biblical blockbuster… so changed has Agadez become through the migrations of many peoples of many races forced to move on by devastating droughts. Once clear of the hustle and bustle I orientated two large maps, weighted their corners with stones on a smooth patch of ground and indulged in vivid memories of former sites to the north-east… wells close to Adrar Bagzane with wonderful names like Efouk Simanti and Tchi-n-Esselemane. I-n-Kouffaouane, as I say, Hydro's first contract in Niger, all of ten years ago now and the furthest east I ever got. Where are you right now, Arambey old mate?, I thought. Dodging the back of my hand a fly persistently returned to alight alongside Adrar Greboun. Something stopped my hand, poised for another swipe. The fly remained perfectly still, then brazenly proceeded to make its way south then east across the sheet… through Tamgak Gorge to the Well of Tchou-m-Adegdeg, then south-eastwards to Arakaou, quenching its thirst, so to speak at the Well of Agamgam before it flew off. I tell you!

To avoid suspicion my food purchases were divided between various stores – small tins of Nescafé, canned vegetables, corned beef, powdered milk, cube sugar – that sort of thing. Boosting carbohydrates, one even had a stock of Heinz baked beans, and for this sweet tooth a tin of Lyle's Golden Syrup. Beneath a large green tarpaulin the station wagon's rear-half soon accumulated a wide assortment of supplies. I bought additional water containers and from another outlet stocked up with Johnnie Walker Red Labels and a few dozen cans of Heineken. To my expenditures I added a fair wage paid to a night guard who in a low profile way kept tabs on the now tightly packed vehicle. Hamouri had come good with a comprehensive set of 1:200 000 IGN maps. His inherited travel guide gave a rough idea, but still in need of first-hand descriptions of the Ténéré I paid a surprise call at the single storey mud-brick house of the guide employed for that initial Kouffaouane project.

Kids kicking a deflated football around a litter-strewn piece of ground send one of their team into the house. Moments later a tall, portly figure grandly attired in indigo and white robes appears at the walled compound's corrugated door. Moussa's dark brown voice greets me

19

with a booming 'Chef! Les activities – bien?' Retirement is treating him well. We cross a sunlit courtyard, in the centre of which there stands a ram tethered to a wooden stump. Goats squabble over a cardboard box. I am introduced to a burgeoning family. Grandchildren everywhere. A young girl in a multi-coloured frock and pink plastic shoes goes ahead of us into the living room carrying a tray of Libyan biscuits and a DDT spray. On one wall there hangs the inevitable print of a Swiss mountain scene. No television set. There are drums, shields, spears, swords, a camel saddle and two Ostrich eggs in a wooden bowl lined with sand. Chai is on its way. Relaxing in black leather armchairs we reminisce over shared experiences. It is easier, a decade on, to see lighter sides of what had at best been a rather strained relationship, in sharp contrast to the mischievous, philosophical style of Arambey who subsequently became an integral part of the Company's varying tasks in central and northern Aïr. I'd always sensed that Moussa viewed our mission with some disdain... an irksome fill-in to the more essential duties of ensuring government convoys made it safely across to Dirkou or wherever. We certainly paid him well for his services. But the purpose of my supposed courtesy call is to glean as much information as possible without letting on – a deception I'm rapidly regretting, for no self-respecting guide will ever condone a single-vehicle venture into untracked desert. Moussa's knowledge of conditions are as wide as the Sahara itself and during the course of our chat I become very much more aware of what I am up against. Am shown photographs of his late father, Senegalese-born Fall Arnaud – one with a 'Minitreks' group, and another holding a framed document stating that in Seventy-Four he'd received three hundred thousand CFA from Public Works for marker-posting the Ténéré. I make my excuses and leave, imagining that soon afterwards guide lifts grandchild on to knee: 'I am not certain of the reason for that visit, little one, for *le Monsieur* now plays a different game, and I am wondering if we will ever see him again.'

Then yesterday afternoon I drove to a large clearing in order to swing Moktar's compass. Rounding a corner on the return I caught sight of Typhoo Diara and Inspector Migraine deep in conversation. No surprises there. After topping up the main tank and making sure every jerrycan of diesel was full, I met up with Hamouri for a last walk around the market, where to purchase bread, fruit and vegetables. My many assorted *bidons* of water were already filled to the brim, totalling around forty gallons. If not for its considerable weight, more would have been loaded aboard. A throng were half-encircling a stoop-shouldered storyteller, sat against a crumbling wall wrapped in his hooded fawn and black striped wool and camel hair *burnous*, the Targui's veil partially concealing what appeared to be milky-blue eyes. Eyes that I nevertheless somehow recognised. 'Tafagag' the old man cried with a theatrical flourish of the hands. The crowd pressed closer, hanging on every word. Hamouri translated from Tamacheq how very long ago the man's father had helped dig the Wells of L'Arbre, then turned and said 'Do you not remember him?, his name is Djaram, the night-watchman you once employed but then had to dismiss for suspected theft. He is now blind.' At that precise moment Djaram's trachoma-stricken eyes appeared to meet mine, his voice now silent – the memory of an altogether inconclusive matter which I'd handled badly returning to haunt me once again. When one of the 'Donnez-moi' gang tried to cadge another pen off me I realised the intensity with which I had been observing the assembled faces, features and mannerisms. Routinely I've felt at home in and an integral part of such scenes, the ubiquitous ever-curious European mingling with another crowded market in yet another African town or village – but here was the difference for come tomorrow when these same people would be gathering for yet more of the same, Ed Lanby from North London will have already gone out on a limb, a chill running down his spine from the incriminating stare of a blind storyteller.

Shortly after dark I checked out of l'Hotel de l'Aïr, destination given as Lake Chad. A complete lie. To forestall any follow-ups I have reserved a room for my supposed return in early February, just over three weeks hence. Driving towards the airfield I pictured each pair of headlights in my mirrors to be those of a dark maroon Peugeot, the henchman of a chain-smoking Inspector of Police with orders to tail me at all costs suddenly realizing that he's about to run out of fuel. Wonderful!!

# TWO

Edmund Lanby's assumption had been correct. Unaware of recent mailbag thefts, Arambey fils de Harouna bided his time in expectation of news from England until, come mid-December and finding it impossible to sit around any longer, he'd ridden north from Iferouane, alone, to greet the birds and animals of Adrar Greboun – a retreat into the desert hastened by frustration at his village's complacency in the face of fresh dangers. On the third afternoon and whilst making a final approach to the plateau-topped mountain he was suddenly held in the grip of a premonition; an impending, critical change of direction, its exact nature and significance not immediately clear. Unusually, there were no camel-herding nomads to be seen who might have provided news of his main concern, Idrissa's whereabouts. No vehicle tracks either to suggest the presence of an FLAA unit with whom his eldest son was reportedly involved.

Seated cross-legged next morning by the shallow bank of his dry stream-bed encampment, threadbare blanket around hunched shoulders, he embraced with open arms the bringer of light's first warming rays, certain that a turning point in his life had been reached. Mid-yawn, Arambey adjusted his faded green cotton *taguelmoust* across nose and mouth whilst the thumb and forefinger of his free hand deftly re-arranged a meagre fire's glowing embers. Within seconds, bubbles emerged from the small red teapot's spout, causing the crimson mound of ash upon which it stood to splutter and hiss. "Yandara", he cried, "Mon ami." His majestic white *mehari* momentarily ceased chewing the cud. "Iheri… Tamudi…", but in a line of trees below the deep shadows of gigantic boulders there was now no sign of his pair of baggage camels that front-foot hobbled had the previous evening been slapped on their rumps to shuffle off in search of juicy tufts of grass. Stifling a further yawn the Targui plopped another chunk of sugar into the pot and flipped its lid shut, pondering his next move. 'In such a short time how things have changed, how fickle people can be', he mused, recalling his widely welcomed prediction of half a year back when storm clouds had indeed gathered over the mountains of northern Aïr bringing desperately needed rainwater cascading down Tamgak Gorge, 'This time I should have perhaps remained silent – those who seek my wisdom and guidance regarding personal matters need not have been so dismissive to my seeing darker clouds still on the horizon, foreseeing imminent conflict amongst our own peoples with the possible deployment up-country of Republican Guards. Violence and much shedding of blood.' He cast a handful of bone-hard dates to his riding camel, wafted away a persistent fly and thoughtfully poked the fire with a stick. 'Kidoo… Kidoo…', a flock of Sand Grouse shot low across the *kori* and dropped to ground, a chill breeze ruffling their feathers as they began to peck the sandy earth like so many clockwork toys. A glass of hot, sweet chai now clasped within both hands, he countered alien uncertainty by reflecting on the fine days of his youth spent accompanying his late father on camel journeys: from their Abelama home to the markets of In Waggeur and Tahoua, exchanging and bartering as they went along – down to Tanout for grain – to Zinder, Goure and across to Nguigmi by the shallow waters of Lake Chad. How when a little older he had joined Harouna's salt caravans that each winter made the return crossings to Fachi and Bilma.

There came a sudden clattering of dislodged stones. Certain that Idrissa together with a group of militants had emerged from some hiding place, Arambey swung round – only to see a Barbary Sheep scramble towards a ridge. Then pause. A *Moufflon à manchettes,* so named because of the cuffs of hair above the animal's hoofs, a magnificent male, long silken hair covering its chest, beautifully curved horns the thickest he had ever seen, eyes aflame, retreating now into the shadows. "So this is why. Now I understand." He reached for his satchel, producing two large brown envelopes: the faded blue Identification Card with its stapled black and white photograph, typewritten place and date of birth given as 'Abelama. Vers 1920' A sheaf of yellowing Hydrological Services and Installations headed paper. The second envelope contained a heavily creased school exercise book, the scratched cover once bottle green, its graph-lined sheets filled with verse. Inspired by his late mother's love of poetry the anthology was in French, the language in which he had excelled at a sponsored *lycee* before in later years going on to teach the school children of Iferouane. He turned quickly to a partially torn page:

'Sur l'Adrar Tamaskaouene pendant...'

On Adrar Tamaskaouene and in my youth
I trapped a fine Moufflon
Whose hide and horns would fetch a high price
In Telouess market.

The Efital was held by one hoof
It could not escape. Could not escape
And as I moved in for the kill
The shadow of a large falcon
Crossed my path.

I looked up into defiant eyes
The eyes of the ensnared animal's mate
Staring down at me
From the rocks above
Burning with fear. And revenge.


"Wallahi!" Arambey dug both hands into the churned ground between his knees, allowing particles as fine as those of an hour glass to then slowly trickle through grey, bony fingers. He wondered if nomadic hunters, as very many years ago he had done, were laying traps on Greboun: leather nooses attached to lengths of wood and placed in known paths made Efital easy prey. Then, as he had long feared, this sighting of a Moufflon as fine as that on Tamaskaouene was followed by the deafening roar of a rogue dust-devil tearing itself through thorn bushes. Exactly as it had been. Back then. Closing his eyes in acceptance of so pre-destined an order of things, wincing to the twist of fate's re-sharpened blade which meant there would now be no reconciliation with his wayward son, he drained the chaipot and scrambled to his feet.

"Kai!" The baggage camels were now visible. "Sai Iferouane!"

In expectation of at any moment glimpsing a bird of prey's silhouette pinned to a blanket of overcast sky he turned south, mesmerized by the lugubrious pace of his mount's broad and muscular hoofs across a desolate landscape. He shook his head slowly from side to side, hieroglyphic scratches in the sand made by gust-blown twigs and thorns re-stating his disbelief that after nothing more than a minor eye infection his wife Aicha's life had suddenly ended in Arlit hospital through criminal negligence of an alcoholic foreign doctor. And on Greboun there'd been no sign of Idrissa and his fellow extremists' whereabouts. With a straightening of his shoulders he lifted an imaginary grandson on to the saddle and in the Kel Owi dialect of the Aïr Tuareg described the unfailing pleasure in scanning the horizon for a herd of Dama Gazelle. Upon reaching the *puit* of Idabdaba he replenished his goatskins, then, when within sight of Pic Adesnou called each bird seen by its Tamacheq name; a taking leave of lifelong friends.

Iferouane he found to be in a state of high agitation, the strife he'd forewarned was indeed coming to pass with factions of rebellious Tuareg reportedly now active close to the frontier with Mali. Between Assamaka and Arlit, tourists were being attacked and their vehicles stolen. Worse still, there were in both senses veiled accusations of his own collusion with the militants: why had he gone north?, certainly not simply to meditate: why absent again from Friday mosque?: can such rumours of Idrissa's engagement in rebel activities be true? And is younger son Mohamet and his family down in Tchintoulous similarly involved?

Early next morning and with profound sadness, his three camels packed with plentiful supplies of chai, sugar, flour, dates and millet grain, Arambey departed his village, orientated now towards the rising sun for what he knew would be his final pilgrimage. The massif he's always delighted in claiming to have been split down the middle by a single blow from his cross-hilted *takuba* is known to him as intimately as the backs of his heavily-veined hands. The schoolchildren he'd once taught had often been urged to understand that Adrar Tamgak was the creation of one enormous mound of crystalline rock that had been forced through the Earth's crust by fault-line upheavals four hundred million years back in the mists of time, its riven scar extending eastwards from their seven hundred metres above sea level mountain oasis home to the point where a three-day gradually inclined trek opened out above the sands of the Ténéré Desert. To either side of the narrow, steep-sided Tamgak Gorge there stood summits one thousand metres higher than Iferouane. Adrar Greboun, to the north, held the honour of being Aïr's tallest mountain with an altitude of around two thousand metres – where, Arambey reflected with a wry smile, a Moufflon's appearance followed by a fierce wind roaring through thorn bushes had signalled the commencement of this ten-day journey to Harouna's grave at Adrar Madet.

Some way short of the first *aguelmam* of Bilumai, in the same ravine down which his predicted life-saving rainwaters had cascaded to the wells and gardens of an Iferouane he would not see again, he dismounted to tie his camels in line for the initial three difficult days ahead to be spent scrambling between and over the gorge's now all-but dry boulder-strewn floor. Drawing alongside a weather-worn protruding nose of a rock which reminded him of his own gnarled features, he slid the exercise book from his *gandoura's* inner pocket:

> He does not wake from his sleep
> Beside the fire.
> His body is wrapped in a blanket
> And roped to a camel
> Which is allowed to roam free.
>
> The madugu is making his last journey
> And the caravan follows
> To where the camel at last couches itself
> Close to the mountain

Where they bury Harouna
My father
Madugu of great taghalams.

Then in the morning
The camel is again set free.

Where it next lies down
They dig the sand for water
For a well in his name
In Harouna's name
My Father's name.


"Mes amis… Yandara… Iheri… Tamudi!" His cry echoed back from the canyon walls. "Matolé!" Preoccupied with his son's virtually certain involvement in violent acts against government forces, Arambey tried to ignore a barrage of taunts from a pack of Olive Baboons high above the gorge. 'Perhaps I should not be surprised', he tried reasoning with himself, 'and be more understanding of Idrissa's rebellious nature. Was not his grandfather once caught up in an earlier Tuareg uprising? Until very recently, did not those from outlying hamlets seek not only my advice but gather around to hear over and over again the story of events that took place towards the end of the First War in Europe?… the charismatic leader Kaossen's ambushing of a Camel Corps platoon of French officers and Senegalese *tirailleurs* making their way back to Agadez… the cruel reprisals that followed when many thousands of people, my parents included, were forcibly evicted from the villages of Tchintoulous, Iferouane, Assodé, Timia and made to re-settle in the southern regions of Tegama and Damergu. Dissidence is in Idrissa's blood… has been ever since he was a child. Allah guide my son back to the path of righteousness… that wherever he may be in two days time he will lay down his arms and join in our country's celebrations with good will in his heart.'

At the water-hole of Aghagha the following midday, Arambey filled two *guerbas*, to the derision of a further gang of *Arubis* barking constantly at this rare intruder's progress up the parched channel of Oued Tamgak – an intensely proud Tuareg elder, cloak billowing to gorge-funnelled blasts of warm air, the embodiment of inherited patience, understanding, mischievous humour and fatalistic wisdom, who now sensed that his ultimate fate lay where it had all begun. On Adrar Tamaskaouene. Who next day was able to himself celebrate the New Year by leading his camels down a dangerously steep path to the *aguelmam* of Eloukouloukane. With more water taken on and his baggage camels now on tighter ropes he climbed atop Yandara to ride due east through a series of low dunes that skirted Taghmert, at its base witnessing a Cheetah give unsuccessful chase to a fleet-footed Dorcas. Rounding Arakau's crab-like claws of boulders and dunes he turned south to Agamgam, filling all six goatskins to capacity and collecting more fodder and firewood. With the eastern wall of Takolokouzet at his back he rode at last out into open desert: "… the caravan follows… to where the camel at last couches itself… ."

It was in the fading light of his tenth day out of Iferouane that Arambey could finally cry greetings to the small trees dotted along a basin of flat, hardened sand at the Neolithic spear-shaped mountain's north-western corner. Cry "Sannu" to a small herd of Dorcas Gazelle hidden in their shadows, as that early January evening he proceeded on round to his usual camping place on the opposite side of Adrar Madet – "… the mountain where they bury Harouna… my Father… madugu of great taghalams."

# THREE

Sunday 12/1/92 07.20 006
Cloudless. Windy. Bonnet spare wheel clamps needed
re-tightening.

Could murder a coffee. Police check-point evaded a few miles back. After much bundu-bashing am sure I've hit the right track, not daring to imagine I've made good my escape for at any moment an army patrol could appear out of the thickets and trees ahead. Or in my mirrors. The best excuse I've managed to come up with if caught trundling along this prohibited route is rather pathetic... sub-contracted to make further inspections of old Hydro Services wells. Huh! Wouldn't it make Migraine's day should this all go tits-up! Don't ever recall having felt so exposed, so ill at ease with deceptions such as these. Find it incredulous, too, this turning a blind eye to the cardinal rule of desert travel. Two Trucks, going solo! The paradox, as I was saying earlier, of that childhood fear of small boats on open seas and an envy, almost, of Moitessier's wonderful achievement and his self-discoveries when totally alone. On the drive out I re-read his book 'The Long Way'. Quote: 'The essential sometimes hangs by a thread – so maybe we should not judge those who give up and those who don't.'

Okay! Let's go! My Michelin XSs the only fresh tyre marks to be seen on this *piste's* soft yellow sands. Arm shielding the sun's direct rays on the pitted 'screen I watch Red-billed Hornbills dip and swoop from tree to tree, always just ahead as though showing me the way. Easy does it, Monsieur Lanby, don't go breaking any springs, just remember that this time you're only a tourist. Bastard!! Frequent shifting of low gears for this first stretch to Kouffaouane… rutted, finger-like probes of a vast system of drainage channels clawing their way free from the Aïr's southern foothills.

And on my right, narrow, deep-furrowed paths, but as yet no sign of a camel train. Praying that I wont encounter other vehicles. In the past I only occasionally saw military convoys to-ing and fro-ing from Dirkou, or a scientific group if not tourists hastening back to Agadez in clouds of dust.

Eyes peeled… one on the immediate horizon, the other on the next pothole. Grossly overloaded. Rear springs look like coat-hangars… fuel, water, provisions, two spare wheels, four sand ladders, one shovel… Shit!

08.25 027 Spotted a cloud of red dust moving rapidly behind a line of trees, heading in my direction, convinced it was the gendarmerie. Yanked the wheel hard right, shuddering to a halt just short of a huge termite mound. What turned out to be a swirling dust devil slammed in to the side of the vehicle and roared on its way. Serves me right!

Track dropping left, then sharp right, following the course of a dry river bed. Exactly as I remember it. Swiftly into low range four-wheel drive. Slowly grinding along a channel of shingle and grit… now hard right up and out of the wadi and back on firm ground, keenly observed by a Chanting Goshawk. Fresh headwind. Track still slow and difficult. Cloven hoofprints where gazelles browsed from bush to bush.

And it was along this stretch that one of our Toyotas once had a burst radiator hose pipe. Towed it all the way back to Moktar's garage.

Ahead, half right... small herd of Dorcas. Belatedly aware of my approach they stand rooted to the spot for longer than they surely know to be wise. Then break into a trot, ha!... characteristically kicking their rear legs high as they spring away to a safer distance... from where they watch this noisy intrusion clatter on past. I raise a hand in apology.

Just realised. Twelfth of January today! How could I have forgotten? Six years yesterday. God rest your soul Yvonne, dearest woman, dearest wife, love of my life. Miss you so much.

First caravan. Six, er no, seven lines... eighty plus camels, way over to the right, making for Agadez loaded with salt.

Drifting in from the right and crossing the *piste* now, smooth-worn interconnecting *azalai* trails. My previous route notes confirm this to be Oued Touriyet, where caravans take on water.

Can't be far to go. More corrugations. Land Rover riding them well.

Yes... here... entrance to the smaller wadi. Duck behind a cluster of tamarisks. Engine cut. Starving!

10.40 072 T/off Kouffaouane
Here again, ten years down the line. No sign of anyone, but the village lies some way off. Good Hydro crew memories.

Baguettes, cheese & tomatoes. Still on edge. Must rest up here in the shade for a while. Unwind a bit, although feel tempted to re–visit the wells & the fine people we came to know through that project. But perhaps not.

Saw a few Bustard on the approach to here, their large wings beating the air with slow downward & sharp uplifts of a conductor's baton.

Elle is again concentrating my thoughts – wondering what she's doing this Sunday morning. My letter of a few days back simply outlined the proposed visit to this spot. No mention of crossing to Djanet – the route & timing of my return to UK clearly of no interest to her now. No mention either, through fear of being seen stark raving bonkers, that a desert fly crawling across a map of Southern Sahara had been sufficient endorsement of my belief that Arambey could well be at Adrar Madet.

From a tree as dead as our relationship appears to be I have gathered four large bundles of firewood, now roped to the roofrack alongside the second spare wheel. Very much the unknown from here on. Hoping for a strong crosswind to cover my tracks.

Knew there was something – forgot to buy more bog rolls. Damn!

Depart Kouffaouane 12.25

Eyes peeled again. Broader horizons. Far less vegetation. North-easterly still. Well marked track. Guesstimating could reach the open desert tomorrow mid-morning, all being well.

Noting on the pad at 13.17 091 miles that pebbles polished smooth by the elements spell Tazolé. Tiny airstrip seemingly in the middle of nowhere. Map shows there's a Well. Must be a village around here somewhere. And now crossing a wide, dry water course. Oued Barghot according to the map.

Back on to north-east again. Clearly marked route. Gravelly. Washboard surface much of the time. Head wind, clouds of white dust billowing out behind. Try to ease my vice-like grip on the wheel... nervous anticipation... dust clouds of a military patrol could suddenly appear over the very next ridge.

Blow me down! Ostrich. Four males, making enormous strides over the wide plain for the safety of a rocky outcrop. To the left the foothills are now less prominent. And yes, it's Lanby the Ostrich speaking... he who prefers to stick his head in the sand rather than hear anymore what the doctor has to say. To date this trip seems to be doing me good.

Cloudless afternoon. More caravan trails, marked by the skeletal remains of camels... heads thrown back... teeth bared in final agony.

I proceed, finally, after the first stick in deep sand. Nearly went through the windscreen as the motor hit a concealed patch of *fech fech*. Much shovelling, positioning and repositioning of all four sand ladders before regaining firm ground... the ladders having in the process become buried deep in gypsum the colour and texture of cement powder. Meaning more shovelling of course. Keeps you fit.

There! A three-line *azalai*... over to my right... forty or so camels... laden with straw and heading for the Ténéré.

Barren, gently undulating terrain. An isolated mountain ahead now, dominating an otherwise featureless horizon. Map and miles covered says it has to be that which Moussa described as having a darkened summit, as if permanently shadowed by cloud.

15.20 128 Adrar Azzaouager
Enough for today. Knackered. Cloudless. Sheltered from a chill easterly.

Large scotch in hand (dimpled glass still unbroken) I watch the sun dip towards the distant Aïr. First Quarter Moon overhead. Strange & beautiful silence whenever there's a lull in the wind. I give Thanks for having safely come this far. No other vehicles. No patrols. My lucky day. As I say, this is what you find.

The mountain's shallow base has made it possible to garage the L/R within a rectangle of some giant's toy building blocks. Well hidden. Impossible to see from the track. Map shows Ad Azz to be around 3,000 ft above sea level = 1,000 ft clear of this expanse of blackish/yellow gravelled sand. Moussa called it Amzeguer.

Conserving water from now on as much as poss. i.e.no washing. Teeth only. Tension now making way to some considerable relief. 128 miles covered today. Feel to be a million miles from civilization. Again reminded of Arambey's oft-given advice 'Believe only the words of the desert wind.'

I again scan this lifeless terrain with my binoculars, but still no sign of that camel caravan seen heading this way.

\* \* \*

Two weeks have already slid beneath the feet of Tazrine fils de Warariz, *madugu* of the three-line *azalai,* since together with his sons departing their home town of Marandet, fifty miles south-west of Agadez. The winter previously he had shared the long trek to Fachi and Bilma with Tourlin and Hassan, fellow Targuis who, no longer possessing the required stamina for another such undertaking, had entrusted their strings of eleven and twelve camels to their old and trusted friend's apprentice *caravaniers.* Upon successful completion of their severe test of character, Agaly and Boubaka would each be rewarded with a camel of his choice, aware that their father's bronchial cough and occasional chest pains were made bearable by the intense pride he felt in introducing them to the traditional ways of salt caravans.

Three days into the march their encampment outside Agadez presented Tazrine with the rare opportunity to make contact with the eldest of his three sons, Bazo, found accompanying a party of tourists around the market. Whilst there he purchased four small bottles of *magani* in the hope of easing his troublesome coughing fits. But now, six days on, and east of Agadez, the cough persisted as he led his caravan into the night. Beyond the Moon's glow a speck of light contrived to avoid each star in its path as it arced towards the horizon. "Apollo" he cried, pointing to the satellite. On his either side at the head of their respective lines of massively laden animals Agaly and Boubaka dozed in their 'saddles' of cross-roped bales of straw – there being no pasture east of the mountains – a sixth sense preventing them from tumbling to the ground. They had soon tired of being cajoled into memorizing important landmarks, happier by far to jealously contemplate brother Bazo's skill at pocketing visitors' handouts and steering clear of arrest. Numb with cold, rocking back and forth to their mounts' vigorous gait, they waited with growing impatience their father's call to make camp for the night.

In an attempt to combat the headwind's knife-edge, Tazrine leaped down and slid his feet into well-worn leather sandals. The lead camel's bell tinkled close to his turbaned head; a brisker stride soon established sufficient pressure on the nose-ring cord to keep his line of sixteen at reasonable stretch. He fingered amulets, clasped a voluminous *gandoura* tight across his chest and recalled recent gratifyingly warm experiences. Touriyet… midday… making their way single file up the wadi… the crunch-crunch-crunch of hooves sinking into heavy-grained sands. Hassi Guessis where *guerbas* were replenished and the camels watered. Then that young Targuia scooping a naked child into her arms and hurrying to her palm frond hut, from where to watch the departing procession rustle past. And, cackling like a hen, the old crone with flat squares of goats cheese grasped between claw-like fingers... her fierce grip not released until he'd parted with a five hundred franc note. 'How alive I feel here in open desert', he smiled behind his veil, 'and if Allah wishes it to be, then ours will be a safe crossing without loss of camels to injury or fatigue. I must not show anger towards my sons, but hope they will carry on the family tradition. The ways of the desert are honourable... there is comradeship here amongst those who ride with an *azalai.*' The stars by which in a few days Tazrine would navigate their way through complex series of dunes began to swim in fluid-filled eyes. He smiled against his pains and concerns, breaking into a chant... sudden recollections of a camel that once stumbled, bursting open a full goatskin of water against a rock... and the replacement bought from a wizened old man who had failed to clean and prevent the skin from producing maroon-coloured water for weeks afterwards.

Coming upon other tracks he stooped to squeeze a pellet of fresh dung between his fingers, peering at the diffused skyline for signs of a camel train possibly five times the size of their own. As he increased his pace a fierce tug of the cord made him whirl round – an agitated beast part-way down his line was on the point of breaking free. Reacting instantly to the screams of command, his sons jumped down and dragged their own columns clear until the panic-stricken animal could be brought under control.

Heaving raucously by now and in need of more cough mixture, reluctantly calling a halt far earlier than planned, Tazrine branched off towards a solitary mountain bathed in sulphurous light which he announced as the very significant landmark of Amzegeur.

"Ssshhhhh... Ssshhhhh..." As each camel see-sawed down on to knees and haunches its twin bales of fodder and double sacks of millet were pushed backwards on to the sand – each constantly bellowing creature then brought back on to its feet to be finally couched and knee-hobbled for the night – straw thrown into the circles of ravenous, teeth-clashing heads.

Their blazing fire is this night one of the very many between Aïr and Kaouar sending sparks of acacia wood spiralling into the clear, moon and starlit sky: brief halts during crossings and re-crossings of vast dune lines, and lengthier encampments at the oases of Fachi and Bilma where bartering and exchanges of grain for pillars of salt are in progress. It is Tazrine's intention that they return with only the finest *kantus* from Bilma's Kalala salt pits to where, he suspects, the larger caravan ahead is making for. And he reflects that such a combined force would, seven or eight decades past, have been considered small and vulnerable to attack by Toubou raiding parties from Tibesti. Back then Telouess, situated beneath Bagzane Massif, had been the assembly point for great Autumn and Spring trans-Ténéré salt caravans – *taghalams* said to have numbered between twenty and thirty thousand camels. As Agaly and Boubaka licked clean their bowls of millet pap, Tazrine recounted such events as once described by Warariz, his late father. There was now no danger of attack and successive government decrees continued to protect *azalais* from any form of motorised salt transportation. But there were dangers still. His scarred forefinger drew crosses in the sand: Balagal... Taharou... Soloto... their progress so far. With a gesture of his veiled mouth he indicated the direction they would in the morning take towards Tafagag, the Tree of Ténéré. He then looked up at the stars: "... Amanar... Corkayat..." And Inaru, the Southern Cross, low in the sky but visible. "The constellations of winter are your friends. Seven days march from here, through high dunes, towards that star... there... you will reach Termit where lives the Hyaena."

After passing their feet and splintered hands through flickering flames his sons disappeared back into the ring of absolute darkness that encircled their fire. Ever attentive to the muffled roars of his restless herd being fed more *alemoz,* Tazrine then prepared another small blue chaipot and pushed it into the pile of glowing ashes. He debated whether or not to test the youngsters' powers of observation: had either of them spotted intermittent flashes of torchlight shortly before they had stopped for the night? And earlier, had they been aware of that far-off *mota*?

Witnessing three silver arrows fire across the heavens simultaneously, Tazrine promised himself that come morning he would describe both the meaning and importance of such a rare moment.

# FOUR

A disturbed night, however, caused him to quite forget his intention to explain the vital significance of triple shooting stars – that somewhere in this desert people had become lost – that a departed *madugu* was returning to Earth and would guide them to safety. Still only partially awake he lowered the veil of his *taguelmoust* to blow hard at the base of their re-kindled fire, then cleared throat and nostrils into the sand. Sat arms over knees and with blankets pulled tight around their shoulders, his sons waited for the water to boil, eyes closed to swirling dust. An inquisitive White-capped black Wheatear fluttered across to the tripod of waterskins. The old Targui nodded his head – the *Mulah Mulah* bird was a good omen.

Third glass of deliciously hot, sweet tea drained, Agaly and Boubaka hurried off to continue preparations for an early departure. Tazrine dropped his two small chaipots and an old biscuit tin packed with tea, sugar, glasses and spoons into a leather sack. About to loop a padlock through its thongs he suddenly doubled-up in pain – similar to that experienced at Soloto. Hands clenched to his chest he glanced around to ensure his sons had not seen what had happened. When at last able to again stand he finished packing his belongings, took another swig of *magani* and kicked sand over their fire.

Working in unison and with soft hide aprons tied around their waists as protection against the sharp-edged straw, they couch and again knee-hobble the first disgruntled beast of burden in front of double bales of *alemoz*. A lead rope is yanked tight over the lower jaw. With Agaly holding its head to the ground, Tazrine and Boubaka place two roped-together leather sacks of millet around the hump, then with enormous effort haul the net-meshed bales over the camel's rump and flanks. As soon as the connecting ropes fall squarely across the bags of grain the hobble is kicked free. Roaring incessantly the animal swings its large frame and enormous, carefully balanced load forwards, on to its knees, rising in two stages up on to the hind legs, then in spurts of sand and dust clambers to its feet, urinating and kicking at its undersides. "Yaaauuuu... .Waaaaaaaa." Faced by a particularly cantankerous creature Tazrine thrusts his hands into the camel's wide open mouth, takes firm hold of its lower jaw and twists the neck ever lower to the ground, forcing the animal to its knees. An un-muzzled beast's attempt to snatch straw from the back of another camel is halted as Agaly throws grit down the culprit's throat.

Tazrine had almost completed the head-to-tail roping of the herd when he noticed a stranger walking towards them. Hastily re-adjusting his head-dress the veil masked a broad grin of satisfaction in knowing all along that they had not been alone. He held out his hand to the tall, grey-bearded European both in welcome and surprise at not seeing other *turists* coming over to take photographs of their caravan. The visitor returned the greeting in both Hausa and Tamacheq, continuing with single syllable words and a waving of arms to convey the purpose of his mission. Tazrine responded in similar fashion, both eventually laughing and shaking hands again at their comical exchanges.

The visitor's departing gift was generous – and when another camel is purchased it would be deemed an honour should it be named 'Eddie'.

"Bis Millah!" With everything loaded and scraps of uneaten fodder collected up, the *azalai* strode out towards the rising sun. After a short while both Agaly and Boubaka clambered up on to their lead animals, whilst their father's sandaled feet slid noisily across firm, orange sands that here and there glistened with a mosaic of shiny pebbles and pieces of broken Ostrich eggshell. He kept pace with the tinkling bell, nervously twiddling the *gris gris* talismans that hung by a leather cord around his neck. Suddenly aware of distant rattlings, way over to his left, he waved an arm of farewell to clouds of dust as the *mota* overtook them again. There followed excited exchanges of opinion, made difficult by a gusting wind, regarding 'Edhey' who had paid a visit and given them many thousands of CFA. Then after a further period of thoughtful silence Tazrine called across to his sons that their next night stop would be on the open sands of the Ténéré – halfway towards which their earlier visitor was now pulling over for his first halt of the morning.

\* \* \*

Snow, as forecast, is turning to sleet in Winchmore Hill, London N21. Snug within semi-detached warmth an arm edges sideways across the bedside table; slender fingers like the jaws of an amusement arcade crane make their pinpoint descent upon lighter and ciggies. Eight-fifty by the hands of an heirloom carriage clock stood proudly on a chest of drawers reputed to be of some considerable value. Best friend Janice phoning at nine. Central heating to be switched to constant once sufficient courage can be summoned up to throw back the bedclothes. With the uncanny resemblance of a wobbly jellyfish a ring of smoke floats towards the Portuguese Man o'War of a lampshade suspended above the brand new John Lewis king-size duvet, its mauve and white pattern etched by slivers of daylight that have succeeded in piercing the drapes of deep golden French windows curtains – the bedroom having remained downstairs from the day Raymond's health had taken a final turn for the worse.

"Hi Jan, nice of you to phone. What's that?… no, have still to venture forth. Am making the most of not now having to work Mondays." Second fag. "Of course I'm alone, silly… can't imagine what you mean. But it was so sweet of you and Neil to invite me to your dinner party. Pardon?… I agree, Philip certainly knows how to tell a story. Yes, by all means pop over for a coffee. Drive carefully. See you later."

Quickly downing sliced banana and yoghurt, still in dressing gown and slippers, boiler chunterring away again, Eleanor Staunton decides against mentioning what less than ten minutes ago happened to plop on to the mat. Is struggling to retain her composure, finding it necessary to clasp the mug of tea between both hands whilst studying a line of colourful stamps marked Republique du Niger. "So you remember my address!"; the hoped-for airmail letter that will remain unopened until… 'Until the inquisition has run its course… bless her… so thoughtful of them to arrange a foursome for this Sahara widow. Philip Armitage is widowed too, it seems. No children either. Now where have I heard that before? No, it was good to feel human again… to have had the luxury of a taxi laid on so I could have a drink. Opportunity to have given the turquoise outfit an airing… stockings, heels dab of perfume. All that. First time in weeks. Yet as soon as Jan arrives all she'll be gagging to know is, was advantage taken of his very kindly running me home? He's a dishy man, Mr P. No denying. Then that moment of weakness when I accepted his invitation to a meal out. Tomorrow! After work. God, what am I going to wear? But it was good to hear his professional views on antique furniture... made a change from the finer points of sand-swept ergs and regs. Later I dared take a look in the wardrobe mirror, didn't I?... MY wardrobe mirror, should you decide to ask, naughty thoughts Janice. And now this airmail letter.' "No, Edmund Lanby, if it wasn't for some sort of likeness to your long departed Yvonne, I doubt you'd have given me a second glance. Crikey, look at the time!!"


Agadez
Tues 7/1/92

Dear Elle,
    Am gutted that you find yourself becoming increasingly angry. Had very much hoped you might fly out here to share the drive back. Meantime a phone call to Iferouane has brought about a change of plan. First off, in a few days time, think I'll drive out to Kouffaouane for old time's sake, as its the site of HSI's first contract in Niger. Hoping to eventually track down my old guide Arambey.

    Take good care

    Edmund x

* * *


Pause for a leg-stretch, having seen just one very large caravan since setting off. It is perhaps an illustration of how much a part of everything I now feel in that I now realise that I didn't take the camera with me when calling on Tazrine and his sons first thing this morning. That was some experience. Okay, had better enter up a few notes.

13/1 NE Add Azz 10.05 018
Got away late. During refuelling I carelessly let the j/can slip from cold hands – perhaps a gallon of diesel seeping

into the sand at my feet. Then as I climbed down from the roofrack I gashed my right forearm on the shovel. Bandage job. Not concentrating.

Twenty minutes ago I hit a pothole with such force that the L/R took off. Nothing broken, amazingly. Distraction again as I attempted a rough count – possibly 250 or more straw–laden camels – the large c/c Tazrine is hoping to catch up with. Tempting fate, but still no other vehicles seen since leaving Agadez. What plausible excuse if picked up this far out? Now beyond another solitary peak shown as Issek–n–Ouggour. The well–defined piste beginning to look like a Clapham Junction of old tracks.

Am about to enter the great void and an idea. One I've been toying with for some time. A change of tack i.e. before turning north for the 90 mile drive to Adrar Madet, think I'll nose my way across to the famous Arbre, or what was the last surviving acacia, apparently, right out in open desert & marked on all maps (Eau très mauvaise à 40m). Moussa explained that a metal Tree, welded together in Agadez, has replaced the fallen original. Looks to be pretty much straightforward. Calculate it as a 70 degrees heading for approx 28 miles. There are bound to be many tracks leading to it. Shouldn't take more than 3 hours there and back & will be a practical test of Moktar's aircraft compass.

Departing 10.20 018.

Going okay, but now... at coming up to twenty to eleven... am having to use low ratio gears as its getting... Merde!. Up to the axles again in cement powder.

Strengthening wind. Have had to put the goggles on. Much laddering.

And on again. Seventy degrees still. The majority of all these old sand-filled tracks now bearing left... the route to Achegour and Dirkou presumably.

Taking a short break alongside a black marker post. One of those put down by Moussa's Dad? Featureless expanse, in every direction, the horizon a white haze where desert becomes sky. The sun now what my old man would have described as dim as a Toc H lamp. Let's read again what the goat-chewed travel guide has to say: 'L'Arbre du Ténéré is believed to have been three hundred years old and the last surviving tree of a tributary of Oued Tafidet that once flowed from the Aïr Mountains out into open desert. In January Nineteen Thirty-Nine and under the supervision of French Army Sergeant Lamotte, native workers dug a Well alongside L'Arbre... two Wells were eventually dug, both now concrete lined. One has a beautiful cathedral-like echo... some believe a vent de sable blew the Tree to the ground, whilst others say it had been felled by a lorry... toppled in Nineteen Seventy-Three it is now on display in Niamey Museum.' Unquote. Even a metal tree, as described by Moussa, should be worth seeing.

On again. Surprised at the compactness of the sand now. A rippled rumbling of tyres. De dang a dang dang... so... so you think you can tell... heaven from hell... havn't had the cassette player out of its poly bag since my great escape. Afraid of breaking the spell. And the pocket tape recorder remains in its case... has been since leaving England. Wonder where Tazrine and sons will camp tonight? Right here maybe.

Ominously, the wind is beginning to lift the sand. Visibility nowhere near as good as it was five minutes ago. The faint tracks I'm following are now at seventy-three degrees. Where are you metal tree? Ha!... might need a magnet instead of a compass. Fifteen miles to go... third gear high ratio most of the time. Bang!... down and across another white rock-hard depression... no sensation of speed whatsoever... and wallop... up on to rippled sand again... gentle undulating waves of a yellow sea.

Three or four miles back I picked up six very fresh tramlines which look to be no more than an hour or two old... three motors heading seventy-five degrees for, or of course maybe having just left, L'Arbre.

Thought I was home and dry, but the sodding tracks and compass have gone and swung through ninety... now a hundred... plus! Dead reckoning's flown out the window.

Christ!!

11.35 044 Fuck knows where I am, but at least the wind is now abating after total mayhem. Have just been engulfed by a ginormous brown wall of sand & dust, the air filled with electricity, grit rattling against the windows like hailstones. The whole of the Sahara seemed to be on the move. Zero viz, out of which loomed an image of Djaram the blind storyteller of Agadez market. Veil lowered. Smile of sweet revenge. Must be going paranoid. Anyway, nothing for it but to double back to the black marker post, pretty quick sharp, now that viz has improved a bit.

Everything secure... okay, here we go... round in an arc, making sure to lock on to my own tracks... no-one else's. What's left of them... half obliterated... disappearing into nothing.

Six miles covered and finally on to two-seventy degrees. My tracks of an hour ago are only visible when I'm right on top of them. Concentrate... concentrate...

I'm now finding it impossible to distinguish which were my outward tyre marks… two-seventy, two seventy… wish to hell it was possible to see further than fifty yards.

Now thumping across a maze of old tracks… third gear low ratio… please don't get stuck, beautiful Land Rover. Foot to the floor… two seventy… two seventy… have to hit the foothills soon…

Rocks! Piles of rocks. Thank God!

Terra Firma! Couple of swigs. No idea of my exact location, but having now crossed that maze of ruts I could well be north of the Achegour/Dirkou route.

Volcano kettle on. Lesson learnt. Arambey, old friend, I now know very well what the winds of open desert have to say.

# FIVE

In the aftermath of the raging, zero visibility *vent de sable* that had swept westwards from Bilma, a crystal clear fresh dawn bears witness to life picking up from where it had left off: at a bugler's call soldiers grab their rifles and rush out on to Fort Dirkou's chalk-white parade ground as the Préfet's armed convoy sweeps in through the main gates – emerging from its grass clump shelter the solitary Addax antelope continues winding its way through the Grand Erg – beneath a certain metal-branched tree purple-grey ticks scurry across dung-strewn sands kicked up by the arrival of a forest of legs, being the considerably larger caravan a father and teenage sons from Marandet have eventually caught up with; who now take their turn to draw water from the least polluted of Tafagag's twin Wells. But life has yet to move on for two Libyan *camions* and their three dozen citizens of Niger returning home from various types of employment in Fezzan, their possessions hung from ropes on all sides, as they strive in vain to un-stick one of the grossly over-laden trucks from a quagmire of *fech fech* west of Achegour.

Its scaly back glistening in late morning sunshine, an inquisitive Darkling Beetle boldly approaches two very dusty boots. "Alexander! Hi. Cheers... your health. So what brings you to this dot on the map? And you might well ask what an old geezer with a limestone coloured station wagon is up to also. You see, this time yesterday Cap'n Pugwash here got disorientated in a mother of all storms that cocked up his dead reckonings. Limped back to port, didn't he, in a real pea-souper. But if that peak over there is Issek-n-Ouggour and I've taken correct bearings then, according to my large scale map, this hillock is named Emekachouar... upon which as you can see, I sit contentedly reading my book and enjoying a drink. Trying to pretend none of it happened. Tell you, came close to being very dodgy indeed. Never thought a barren mound of boulders such as these could be so welcome a sight. And what's the rush? Madet will still be there tomorrow... old Arambey too, with luck. But right now I'm in the excellent company of your good self, and Mr Wheatear perched on the tent waiting for the remainder of the breadcrumbs. Have had my first hot meal in three days and the gashed forearm is beginning to heal nicely. Still taking the artery flow tablets and havn't lost my marbles. Yet! Will again check the motor, make sure everything's shipshape, then weather permitting I'll be heading north in the morning. And you, Alex... what are your plans? Oh, I see... making for those foothills. Take good care, there are Ravens about." Tiny legs scraping a path between the pair of ridge-soles became en-shadowed by a journal opened for further self-reflection.

A beetle pauses to say bon jour. Politely listens to my show of bravado. No, that all-encompassing void twenty four hours ago severely tested my resolve – showed how easily one could become crushed by the weight of a surrounding sweet f–all. Added to which am continuously aware that I'm contravening a no–go–area – shouldn't be here at all – breaking all the rules. Part of me has been saying hold your hands up & trundle on back the way you came, the counter–argument being that that storm & a half was a blessing in disguise.

For drawing ever closer to L'Arbre I'd given up caring whether or not there'd be a military patrol sat under the Tree listening to their trannies – which could have seen

Two Trucks Lanby being escorted back to Agadez to try a pair of handcuffs on for size courtesy of a chain-smoking Inspector of Police – my having blown this once in a lifetime chance to perceive what lies beyond.

Each and every moment of his long life has been lived to the full: caravanier, teacher, parent, guide, mentor to young and old alike. Accomplished hunter too, once, of *Moufflon à manchettes.* Now, sub-consciously fingering the sand between his knees Arambey fils de Harouna, 'date de naissance vers 1920', believes retribution awaits but a short while hence. He prods mauve tongues of flame fanned by a light breeze, the green and white striped sand-encrusted blanket over his shoulders evidence of *la tempête* which the day previously had swept through his temporary camp, half a day's ride north-east of Adrar Madet. His three camels have now laid bare this patch of ephemeral pasture: one more chai, therefore, before setting off back. As it comes time to kick loose gravel over the fire he is reminded of their arrival at Madet a week ago – the climb to his lookout cave with small pyramids of blown sand at its entrance suggesting that over the preceding twelve months no rare visitor had discovered and occupied his partially concealed hideaway – then the second scramble high above a rock overhang to the hidden *guelta* familiar only to him, this time found to contain more than enough rainwater for an extended stay. He becomes mindful of the first of his many pilgrimages to his father's grave, located nearby, when in search of water he had ridden the full length of both sides of the narrow mountain, his reconnoitre taking from dawn 'till nightfall. Every January and whilst employed by Hydro Services he had requested special leave in order to... "Mes amis!... I am suddenly aware that my friend Eddie is here again in Niger. Of this I am certain. Kai!"

A final backward glance to ensure nothing has been left behind. Sandaled feet then slide easily over a compacted surface, loose-fitting trousers and robes flapping loudly in a freshening north-easterly that like cold hands press against aching shoulder blades. Without slowing his animals' pace he pulls Yandara's jaws close to the ground, hooks one knee over a broad neck, releases tension on the lead rope and as the head is raised clambers up on to a saddle of sacking and blankets. "Yeeeaaoouu... Ina gajiya?... Lafiya?... Lafiya lau... "

Arambey allows his body to rock to and fro in exaggerated fashion, chanting and rejoicing his former team leader's return in rhythm to the pad-pad-pad of his camels' feet and the sloshing of what water remains in the goatskins. His mount's nonchalant stride pleases him – yet is a joy tainted by memories of no more to be seen Scimitar-horned Oryx and Addax antelope that many years past might have been spotted galloping for the safety of the nearest dune. Approaching Madet he scrutinizes the ground for signs of fresh tracks, human or otherwise, then studies the smooth sand directly ahead. As he does so a dagger-shaped silhouette cuts across his line of vision. He winces, lips pursed, teeth clenched in the stark realization that it is now too late – too late to welcome his friend back – this being the final, fateful sign. His camel's neck receives an unusually sharp kick as the raptor circles low overhead – the migrating Honey Buzzard, its strength renewed by carcass scraps after, far from the moist savannas of Cameroun, having been swept by great turbulence ever westwards – a bird of prey's ominous shadow, exactly as it had been when he'd once slaughtered an Efital simply for its hide and horns.

From a vantage point above the cave, come evening and for the last time, Arambey sat watching the sun dip behind far-off Takolokouzet – beyond which he could picture Oued Imaghlane, Taghmert, Tamgak and Iferouane. And *le jardin* which would soon pass into his sons' possession. Way beyond that, Adrar Adesnou, where many times he had listened to icy cold winds announcing the arrival of winter. 'Madet… these sands all around… I know so well, and in turn feel to be known.' The thought induced a stoic smile: the day following their arrival he had wandered with his grazing camels towards lines of low dunes where, relaxing on the floor of a narrow *ghassi*, he'd buried both hands deep into refreshingly cool sands, only to throw himself backwards with a startled cry when his finger-tips encountered something directly beneath where he sat. "Yes, I am familiar with every rock and every dune, and with a Horned Viper's place of hibernation… but in the morning I must leave."

In no doubt as to the direction in which he would be led, he delved into a pocket for a pencil and turned to the next blank page in his school exercise book:

> Je vous dit Adieu
> Mais bientôt, mon ami
> Vous suivrez…

In swiftly fading light he made his way down. All six goatskins were filled. Adequate supplies of millet and camel fodder remained for the three days south-westerly ride to Oued Tafidet. Final respects had been paid at Harouna's grave; just the camels to be fed and knee-hobbled for the night. Gazing into a cloudless sky bathed in quicksilver he listened with all his being for the remotest chance of an approaching vehicle, before resignedly climbing slowly back up and across to lookout cave.

An unpleasant odour of stale water had earlier this day greeted the now combined *azalai* as it reached Tafagag. Two

Ravens which had maintained contact since Azzaouager peeled away to settle on L'Arbre's rusty boughs, from where to watch and wait. Instructions from Tazrine to his sons were that their own lines should not be allowed to couch themselves in a place littered with the bleached bones of creatures too exhausted to raise their massive frames back up again on to their feet. Three hundred and fifty and more animals idly thumped their undersides to repeated attacks from an army of very determined camel ticks whilst, to triumphant cries and the squeaking of forty metre lengths of rope on wooden pulleys, leather buckets of splashing, sparkling water were hauled into the light of day. *Guerbas* only, the herd next to be watered at Fachi. Once all the bulging, shiny wet goatskins had been slung beneath bales of straw, forty fathers, uncles and sons led their respective columns further into the Ténéré.

There soon appeared an Agadez-bound caravan packed with salt, its fatigue measured by lead ropes that were at full stretch. A figure made his way over, clutching half an inner tube into which someone transferred a contribution of *Eau de Labara*. Then a negroid lad who looked half their age ran across to Agaly and Boubaka, sweat shirt down to his knees, feet dragging a pair of man-size shoes through the soft sand, as for a few minutes he chose to walk alongside the large camel train, back the way he'd just come. Ailou's eyes were red, the surrounding skin swollen. Shivering, a blanket clutched around his neck, he spoke of fierce sandwinds and a longing to reach home, before turning to chase after his fast disappearing lines.

Shortly before dusk Tazrine joined others to face Mecca and kneel in prayer. He had instantly acknowledged a fellow Targui as *madugu machaou* – overall leader – who in turn was taken aback to see such a marked change in his friend's health. "Thank you Baluto, but I have enough *magani* until we get to Bilma."

Beneath the beacon light of a Moon now a matter of days from Full and as though a formidable raiding party stealing up on an enemy through complexities of overshadowing dunes, shoulders are hunched to a biting wind, faces covered by cloth against crest-blown sand. Two teenagers rapidly becoming men in a baptism of endurance and pain cling benumbed with cold to their bales' cross-ropes awaiting Baluto's final command to drift back over the shuffling herd's grunts and sighs, the screekings of jaws chewing cud and the constant shee-shoo, shee-shoo, shee-shoo of baled fodder.

# SIX

Beneath the few days off Full lunar light and contrary to expectations, a cloud pattern threatening more snow having now dispersed, driving conditions for those venturing along country lanes north of the M25 this dark and cold mid-winters evening have become marginally less hazardous. He indicates left and noses his Range Rover into the Hunting Horn's car park. The couple crunch across a gravelled yard to the threshold where, relieved of overcoats, scarves and gloves, they are shown through to the pub's tastefully refurbished dining area. Once seated, a candle on their reserved table is lit. Menus and wine list in hand, he exchanges driving for reading spectacles.

"What a pleasant get-together that was at Janice and Neil's the evening before last."

"It was indeed. Jan and I were colleagues at Chase Farm for many years. Ten, we reckon, on the Admin side, and have remained in touch ever since."

"Hospitals scare me. As you know, Neil and I were at the same university, our re-making contact about a year ago when my opinion was sought regarding that fine Grandfather clock in their hallway. Elle, I believe you said that you were interested to establish the provenance of a certain chest of drawers." Belying his fifty-nine years the tanned, silver/grey haired authority on Nineteenth Century collectables is seen by his dinner-date as elegance personified: Expensive suit. Flamboyant tie. 'Dishy man'.

Between starters and main course Eleanor Staunton discovers the Pinot Noir to be to her liking also. Now on the subject of travel their anecdotes and laughter are clearly riling a cheerless couple on the adjacent table. Philip's turn again:... group stranded halfway up the Atlas Mountains with a guide who's afraid of heights...

Concealing a yawn she suddenly wishes they were not discussing Africa. 'Hardly got a wink of sleep last night, having eventually got a call through to that hotel in Agadez. What can Edmund be up to at Lake Chad? If alone. If not with some Bardot look-alike from the French Embassy.' "Er, forgive me for interrupting Philip, but in addition to Morocco would I be correct in saying that you have also visited West Africa?"

"How extraordinarily perceptive of you, my dear."

"Lake Chad by any chance?"

"No. Burkina Faso and Mali are the regions I have tended to concentrate on mostly. Ouagadougou... isn't that such a wonderfully outrageous name for a country's capital? Bamako less so, I fear, compensated for by other charms. In Mali, particularly, there exist a wide variety of cultures that draw me as a moth to a flame. You may be aware that the star Sirius plays an enormous part in Dogon folklore."

"Has your itinerary included Niger?"

"Alas, Niger I have not yet had the pleasure of visiting... a country bearing the name of the river down which in the early Eighteen Hundreds Mungo Park, mistakenly, went in search of the source of the Nile. But I've an inkling as to why you ask. Prior to you and I being introduced, Janice and Neil took the precaution of putting me in the picture… you see Elle, I have a reputation for careless gaffes."

"Don't we all."

"Eleanor, if I may be so bold. Would I be correct in believing that you now find yourself cast adrift upon a very cruel sea?"

"Walked out on me. And!… and, would you Adam and Eve it, his late wife's first name happens to be my middle name. Yvonne. Still lets slip an Evie when he's had one too many. Or did, I should say."

"No news since, presumably?"

"A letter has now reached me. Finally. After much thought I put a call through to Agadez. Last night in fact. Hotel reception have never heard of a place called Kooffwane… something like that… and I can't find it on any map. In any case they inform me that Monsieur Lanby has gone to Lake Chad and is not expected back, in Agadez that is, for another three weeks. Room reservation made for the third of February."

"Kooffwane you say… a place with which I am as yet unfamiliar."

"Might give the consulate a ring. Am considering flying out to Niger. Swallowing of pride and all that."

"Splendid though this idea may sound, my dear, it is an enterprise that will first require considerable thought, for should you arrive in tropical Africa only to discover that of Monsieur Lanby there is neither sight nor sound, will you not therefore find your beautiful self at some risk…"

"I'll fly straight back to London."

"… at some quite considerable risk, I would venture to suggest. Alone and vulnerable in an uncivilized country, not unlike those intrepid Victorian explorer ladies , in fact, who allegedly beat restless natives over the head with their gamps."

"I just so happen to possess a gamp. Family heirloom. Antique, like my chest of drawers."

With their entering the warm and spacious living room cum museum of his luxuriously converted single storey farm building on the outskirts of Enfield, he is barely able to restrain his delight on hearing his guest's appreciation of the subtle lavender and dove-grey decor: "Philip, I simply adore this room." Is thrilled with this opportunity to conduct a short guided tour: "That fine wood carving of an antelope is in fact a Kurumba mask. Over here we see an excellent example of a Dogon millet granary door. Either side of those bookshelves there stand a selection of other masks found in West Africa." He is pleasantly surprised, also, that the warm and tender hand being led into his world of ethnological art forms remains contentedly in his, having feared an adverse reaction to the display of macabre masks worn, in so many instances, at ritual burial dances. Eight years, now, since Madge took that fatal tumble down a flight of escalators in Dorothy Perkins. "I'll make those coffees we promised ourselves. Please do make yourself at home."

A clock strikes eleven. From a concealed sound system there are heard upbeat riffs from a jazz combo. Foot-tapping exchanges between piano and tenor sax. 'Just one more hour, Cinderella Eleanor. Nothing more to drink. Promise? Must look a wreck.'

Theme music now from 'Out of Africa'. "Classic, Elle, are they not?" From behind, hands align her hips towards a pair of framed prints hung above the cushioned sofa.

"Yes Phil, they are indeed. A smaller copy of Vettriano's 'Waltzers' hangs in my sitting room. Raymond and I loved ballroom dancing."

"Over here… dosn't that Ansell Adams black and white enlargement capture so perfectly the raw beauty of mountain peaks and steep sided valleys held in the grip of an Alaskan winter?"

A chiming of the half hour. 'No.Philip Armitage, keep your hands off. Bastard, you know I fancy you don't you… but no way, even though Edmund is very likely flirting with some ex-pat bimbo by the shores of Lake Chad…'

"Magnificent. Huge."

'Exactly what Eddie used to say when he got his mitts…' "Philip! No! I'd be most grateful if you would now run me home."

"Of course, but might you be agreeable to our meeting again?. Up in town. Do an art gallery. Bite to eat?"

"We'll have to see."

"Here's my card. I have been given to understand that Tate Modern are planning a season of Vettrianos."

# SEVEN

Six and a half hours later and before hurrying off to work, Eleanor Staunton snatched a few moments to flip through the pile of now very familiar photographs of places and people she would have expected to encounter had not her partner's heart scare persuaded her against their together taking a couple of thousand miles return drive down memory lane. Hastily selected prints from Ed's many hundreds of slides were quickly popped into her bag – Agadez minaret, Well-digging at Kouffou-something or other, guides Moussa, Hamouri and Arambey, and a shot of the Hotel de l'Aïr which, as she headed up on to The Ridgeway in her Ford Fiesta, was this very morning being held siege to police investigations.

From the shadows of buildings opposite the Hotel's entrance an ageing silversmith, together with members of the cigarettes and chewing gum gang, are studying the uniformed officers' every move. Rumours starting to circulate: foreign tourist being sought for questioning – Inspector Maïga's patrols to broaden their search – very soon the fugitive will be behind bars. Deep in thought, Hamouri makes his way back to the market square. 'If it is you they seek, Eddie, then by now you will have already entered open desert. Each day Tinna and I pray for your safety. Allah be with you.'

"Testing… Testing. It is ten o'clock on the morning of Wednesday the fifteenth of January. Estimate my position to be at a rocky

outcrop on the south-eastern foothills of the Air Mountains."
**Stop Rewind Play** 'Testing… Testing. It is ten o'clock on the morning of…' **Stop Rewind.**

Good to know it still works okay, this Olympus Pearlcorder, as it could come in handy sometime soon. And what a beautiful calm day, here on the sea shore. No prizes for guessing who had one too many Scotches last night. Sunrise was superb, lifting clear of the flat, featureless horizon like a proverbial red balloon. There was a touch of dew, but the flysheet quickly dried out. In dismantling the tent I noticed a large brown scorpion at my feet, that had sought a warm spot for the night. Soon sobered me up!

Emekachouar 15/1 10.15am
Fresh logbook, appropriately, to commence this next phase of my journey. Already I feel to be a different person to yesterday, where a 'day off' was very necessary, allowing me time to get things back into perspective. To get a grip of myself, basically, for I'd come close to throwing in the towel. Thought the Tree would be a doddle – that after many winters of projects I'd sussed the Sahara. Over-reacted. Tried to dictate events (typically) over which I'd lost control. The trick is to strike an equal balance between positive self-confidence and absolute respect for the desert's unwritten laws and rules. As my natural instincts gain freer rein, so I'm discovering how consolidation & the maintaining of basic routines is so essential – like brushing one's teeth, saying one's prayers, & of course at all times knowing where one is at, in such a potentially hostile environment. Lessons being learnt all the time. Quite different sets of values, now, compared even to those I set out from Agadez with. Yes, I'm contravening rule number one by driving solo into the desert, but how else can I experience 'Beyond Recall' à la Moitessier? Right now, for example, there is complete & utter silence like never before. At sunrise I felt to be a participant in the birth of this new day – & the indefinable

atmosphere (a taboo subject, strangely, in most travel books I've read) of a Presence. Providence.

For the record: 197 miles covered since Agadez (including the 50 miles abortive search for l'Arbre). Charted course: 85 miles to Adrar Madet, 220 across to join the balised Chirfa piste, 190 final run-in to Djanet = 495 miles still to go.
Fuel: calculate on doing 12 mpg (originally estimated 10mpg). Approx 17 galls of diesel used to date out of the 74 galls started out with = 57 galls in hand to cover the remaining 495 miles.
Red j/can of engine oil about three-quarters full.
Provisions for a month.
Water: can never have sufficient – being used as sparingly as poss, for obvious reasons, there being few Wells between here & Djanet. Approx 5 galls consumed = 35 galls remaining. With no puits or aguelmams at Adrar Madet, according to the large scale map, how many goatskins must you have taken with you on your annual pilgrimages, Arambey?

Who, even as Lanby writes his former guide and translator's name, has halted to re-tighten Yandara's saddle and check both baggage camels' loads – again aware of the shrill, impatient cry of the bird of prey circling overhead, its south-westwards trajectory leading inexorably to Tafidet and Adrar Tamaskaouene.

Planetary distances early last evening, when before a guaranteed decent night's sleep in the tent I lay watching the stars of mid-winter come into brilliance as a four-fifths moon rose into the sky. Pleiades, Aldebaran, Orion, Sirius. Southern Cross clearly visible. No satellites seen. And yes, at sun-up had a bit of a scare when the binoculars picked up a convoy, to the south-east, heading not in my direction but away from the Aïr, thankfully. Four tiny black insects bravely venturing into the vast unknown.

No further sign of Alexander beetle. We had a good chat yesterday. Loneliness can manifest itself in such varied ways. At breakfast, earlier, and with Yvonne in mind (having unbelievably forgotten the 6th anniversary of her passing) I played my first cassettes since departing Agadez – Dvorak's 3rd Sym & Beethoven's Violin Concerto. How incongruous they sounded initially, then apt choices for this corner of desert where the Aïr's foothills dissolve into Ténéré sands. Wish very much, Evie, that you could have shared all this. Maybe you are. How vigilant of you to ensure that I have not abandoned my plans. What courage you displayed throughout those final months. At times such as this I realise that we have yet to be parted.

Everything secure. Rubbish buried. Nothing left behind. Hope you're there, Arambey old mate. Put the kettle on! Here we go then... departing Emek six minutes past eleven. God grant a safe passage to Adrar Madet.

Out and away. Blinding sun through the pitted windscreen. Coaxing the heavy vehicle round until the dashboard compass swings on to thirty-five degrees. There! Now to maintain this heading as constantly as poss.

Flat sands, feeling good and firm. Thought of lowering the tyre pressures with the maps showing dune lines ahead, but in the end have left them as is. With each gallon of fuel used the motor loses weight. Calm, cloudless day. Good visibility. Estimating roughly forty-five miles to Areschima Sud, pinpoint of a landmark shown on the large scale IGN map as 'Tombes', five hundred and ten metres above sea level.

Foothills receding to my left... distances difficult to judge. Bugger-all to my right. Third gear high ratio, and now top... thirty mph... eyes peeled for patches of fech fech. Smooth sands, yellow here, orange there… feel to be floating across the desert with little sensation of movement or speed. No other vehicle tracks, new or old. Watching out for arrowhead tracks of Dorcas gazelle. Expecting the unexpected. Now skirting an isolated area of crescent-shaped Barchan dunes. Still very much on the edge of it all, yet feel to be the first person to have ever come this way.

Thirty-five degrees still. Low dune lines to my left now. Fourteen miles on the clock… allowing the motor to roll to a standstill. Engine left running. Don't need this anorak now. Strolling around the Land Rover. Everything okay. A more leisurely pace this time, unlike the Tree when I got out of sync with my surroundings, and myself. Feels right this time. Quick slash and on again.

Back there I think I passed a grinding stone. Read a description of this region being like a sort of open museum, the ever-shifting sands exposing, covering, exposing again all sorts of Neolithic artefacts. The wing mirrors show plumes of dust being kicked up as we cruise along. Twenty miles, approx, to this landmark called Areschima Sud. Wonder what to have for lunch.

And this is how I hoped it would be… totally self-reliant, dependant on my initiative and decisions should the push come to a shove, Completely new territory for me, this, alone yet in a strange way not altogether alone. Difficult to explain… leading to the realization that only Hamouri and Tazrine know very roughly where I am right now.

Areschima Sud? 12.20 042 Could have been the star dune with rocks on its summit that I passed a mile back. Am in a widely spaced system of relatively low SW/NE dunes, just over half−way between Emek and Madet.

Engine switched off. Deafening silence. Lunch of vache qui rit & biscuits. No wind to listen to today, Arambey, just a light north–easterly breeze. Earlier, clumps of grass behind which spear–shaped mounds of sand had piled up indicated, weather–vane fashion, the direction of the last vent de sable.

A continued tack of 35 degrees cannot fail to hit Madet – judging from the IGN its a 12 miles long solitary mountain averaging a height of 500–600ft.

Ignition. Contact. Beautiful... the throaty roar of a diesel engine firing into life. You won't let me down, will you, faithful Land Rover.

Good fast progress across flat sands again. But now, fifty-four miles on the clock, am entering narrower corridors... rolling topped walls of sand to either side which I guess to be on average thirty or so feet high.

Wow! That was a ...'king close shave... gunned the motor up an incline, aiming for what appeared to be an escape route between converging dunes... became disorientated by a shimmering glare of sand and sky, then before realising what was happening felt the front wheels thump over an acute drop, the vehicle slewing this way and that to the base of the cross-dune. Upright. Just. So very close to tipping on its side. The rollicking I've just given myself will have been heard in Niamey!

Took ages to ladder the L/R out on to firm sand. Just climbed a star dune – binoculars picked out what has to be Adrar Madet, directly ahead – a great grey battleship lying at anchor beyond this small sand sea, about 17 or 18 miles away according to miles covered. Whilst on top of the dune a movement way over to the left caught my attention. Two moving objects. Three. One again.

Disappeared before I could get them in focus. Can only assume they were gazelle bobbing between dune crests. Could have been the incredibly rare Scimitar-horned Oryx – nice thought anyway.

Seen from on high the L/R, no bigger than a Dinky Toy looks hopelessly inadequate against the lie of the land – the immeasurable scale of this formidable desert.

All being well, should reach Madet at around . . My WATCH has stopped!! Don't believe this – didn't think to fit a new battery before leaving UK, for it has to be that. Damn! Goodnight Dead Reckoning navigation!

At last, the waves of sand are beginning to part… broaden out. Bit of a roller coaster ride now, down on to and out across an expanse of flat, firm, darker sand.

Seven or eight miles still to go… Madet looking like one enormous burial mound topped by rocks that shine like molten lead in the afternoon sun.

Aiming for the north-easterly corner. Head out of the half-open door… the Michelin XSs forming white tramlines across the dark plain. Listening to their quiet purring.

Hello!… performing a three-sixty. Yes, fresh camel tracks… look to have been three or possibly four camels… heading away from the mountain. I'm now scanning the horizon in the direction from which I've come, but no sight of camel or man.

Quick stop to chuck a whole load of dead branches on to the roofrack.

On again, continuing slowly towards the far corner… retracing these very recent tracks through scattered trees…

... and around the top... to Madet's more sharply inclined side.

Away to my left the sand appears lightish green. Have seen this before... means, by the looks, there's been a spell of heavy rain here not too long ago.

Here! Here the camels were couched. And this fire's embers are still fractionally warm.

Arambey... have I gone and mistaken you and your camels for a herd of Oryx?

# EIGHT

Je vous dit Adieu
Mais bientôt, mon ami...

This has been quite a discovery, I tell you :

So I say farewell
But in time my friend
You will follow
Curious to know
As indeed I am curious to know.

First verse translation from something stumbled upon yesterday afternoon when, after arriving at this area where camels had been couched, I scrambled up loose scree for a view from the top, willing Arambey to be somewhere around still. A fairly tough climb, and a good test of the old ticker. Trips proving beneficial for my ills. It's a boulder-strewn ridge summit, a few hundred feet above a carpet of dark sand and the dozens of small acacia trees I'd passed on my approach, where dry water courses snake their way down Madet's shallower western face. Map-orientating myself I could determine Erg Brusset's waves of yellow dunes away to the north-west. Scattered dunes lay in the opposite direction. Then in making the sharp descent back to the Land Rover I spotted recently trodden patches of sand, which led to a cave-like recess. Wood chippings. Fire-blackened rocks.

Dusty floor with imprints of Tuareg sandals. And this green, rather battered old note book. Next verse :

> So tread carefully
> These rocks possess life
> And death.
> Be not tempted
> By their treasures and secrets.

Just an old school exercise book, but crammed with anecdotal records of defining moments in an eventful life... from camel journeys to wildlife hunting to family and to the burial of his father, Harouna. Therefore these have to be Arambey's writings, this farewell poem meant, I believe, for me... for as such a valued possession this anthology cannot have been left behind accidently. That he somehow knew I'd be coming out to Adrar Madet astounds me... although Arambey never was just your average wise old Targui. There's a rather amusing piece describing 'la folie' of noisy mopeds roaring around the streets of Arlit in the middle of the night. Finally:

> Listen well, therefore,
> To the desert wind
> And if it should be
> Then go quickly
> Even before the gazelles
> Who have no rendezvous

With a prod of his fire's ashes Arambey brews more chai, two days south-west from Madet and still short of Oued Tafidet. He envisages how it will be next morning: his camels' feet scrunching deep into the dry river bed of grit and pebbles – a tug of Yandara's nose cord bringing them to a narrow *kori*, its slight incline bordered by shrubs and calytropis plants.

To well-tended *jardins* of ripening corn and an assortment of vegetables. To pallets of tomatoes laid out in the sun to dry. And to the *Mulah Mulah* bird perched overhead his hand will be raised in salute. A short way ahead will be heard the squeakety-squeak of leather buckets being raised from the deep Well, whilst close by those tall, elegant Targuia stick-tap their bristle-maned donkeys towards a thorn compound. Startled by the Honey Buzzard's dagger-shaped shadow the young girls will glance over their shoulders as a proud figure riding his white *mehari* enters their tiny hamlet of Tilichine. 'I shall not wish for my visit to be remembered with sadness, but from their *puit* my goatskins will have to be filled for my continuing on to Tamaskaouene.'

Snug in his sleeping bag alongside half a dozen crumpled beer cans, Lanby contemplates the old saying that where there's a problem there'll invariably be three, all coming along at once like buses. 'Wouldn't mind being on a double-decker right now, on my way into Enfield Town for a pint in the George. First-off, how the hell did we miss one-another?. Second – my watch has definitely had it... not an issue at the moment but could jeopardise things later... providing, thirdly, that the Radweld does the business.' It had come as a considerable shock, late afternoon, to discover water to be dripping from behind the front bumper. 'As I always say, it's impossible to carry sufficient. Equates to the time one has left. Just hope to God the radiator doesn't burst when I set off for Djanet in the morning... otherwise all's looking shipshape. I pray for a smooth, safe passage northwards.

Against a background of raucous bellowings and snarling neck-fights, two camel-riding days to the south-east of Lanby's lunar-shadowed mountain, Tazrine and his sons sit cross-legged within a wide circle of similarly blazing fires and cooking pots.

"Agaly, do you know which stars have guided Baluto since we left Labara?"

"Yes father. Those two... there."

"Boubaka, in which direction does Bilma lie from here?"

"In that direction, father."

"Tomorrow, my sons, we will reach Fachi, in'shallah."

"Shallah" "Shallah."

Within an amphitheatre of high dunes, voluble exchanges between *caravaniers* compete to be heard against a cacophony of cud-chewing gurgles and grunts. Boubaka resumes his pounding of pestle and mortar – the preparation of millet gruel for the day ahead – a thud, thud, thud reverberating through compacted sand like muffled cannon-fire.

Adrar Madet Fri 17/1 Dawn. Calm clear day
    Moment of truth. Will the radiator hold? But before setting off, something tells me that I should scramble up on to the ridge one more time for a binoculars check on the easiest route out.

Mid morning: A second, priceless gift from Arambey!! From a vantage point a little further along the ridge I first scanned the surrounding desert prepared to be only too glad if dust clouds of even military vehicles had appeared at the eleventh hour. Then magically, a familiar sound. I looked across in time to see a Sand Grouse fly behind a spur of large boulders that seemed glued to the scree-face like some enormous hooter. Curious, I cautiously picked a way down & across to where the bird had vanished – then as quickly re-appear with glistening droplets trailing in its wake as like an arrow it flew back out across the desert. I stood mesmerized, recalling once having read that Grouse are known to raise their young as far away from danger as possible, carrying moisture back to the nest in their breast feathers. The cleft between the two huge slabs of rock was just wide enough to squeeze through. Shafts of light from above revealed what I found to be a translucent pool of water!! slightly brackish yet nevertheless drinkable. I now understand the reason behind a secretive smile & evasive response when HSI crews used to press Arambey for a description of his pilgrimage mountain. How bloody marvellous to have been led to his guelta of rainwater.

By mid-afternoon a square of level ground is beginning to resemble an aid agency base camp: orderly lines of diesel jerrycans and water containers, sectioned-off areas for ammo boxes of spares and tools, a small stack of tinned & dried food, two bundles of firewood collected at Kouffaouane plus dead branches picked up shortly before arrival. A suitable patch has yet to be chosen for the ridge-poled tent. Fresh rubbish hole already dug. Stripped bare, practically, the Land Rover has been nosed close to the foot of Madet and the natural shelter of a protruding slab of rock. He smiles, savouring a bonanza of perfect reasons to lay back and laugh like a loon. Still too early, just, for an appropriate celebration.

Forgot to enter up that this morning, when stood on the ridge of this 12 (bakers dozen) miles long crusty baguette, I discovered that I am not alone! – 5 Dorcas Gazelle spotted amongst the trees on the opposite side from here – whilst the ramparts of Takolokouzet, due west, appeared on this fine viz day to be much closer that 40 or so miles away.

Give or take, have 28 galls of beautiful Agadez water still – marked with green tape. Have just filled a container from the guelta, adding purification tablets, & to of course boil whenever making hot drinks & meals.

Water – with all the time in the world now to set about exploring this proverbial desert island.

Pursuing their ever-lengthening shadows on this Friday afternoon and fourth day east from the Tree of Ténéré, *le caravan du sel* pauses again for prayers. The cliffs behind Fachi have been visible for some while – very soon *la Palmeraie* will come into view. Tazrine kneels, wipes face and arms with both hands, then smoothes the patch of ground that will receive the touch of his forehead. Intoning passages from the Koran he finally accepts a painful reality: 'If by tomorrow evening my strength has returned, then we will complete the crossing, with Agaly and Boubaka setting off back with Bilma's finest salt, in'shallah, but if the *magani* does not ease this cough and pains in the chest, then *forchis* and *kantus* of inferior Fachi salt it will have to be.' Feet slid into sandals he hurries to rejoin the camel train now negotiating another barrier of converging dunes.

It is also *madugu machaou* Baluto's intention to journey onwards from Fachi, but regrets still '… that I cannot be called Hadj. And it is now unlikely that I ever will be. Yet always when entering Le Grand Erg de Bilma I experience fulfilment… those three days will again become my Mecca…

more important even than the arrival in Kalala salines and reunions with old friends.' He glances back – the kid goat perched atop one of his camels nibbles contentedly still at the bale of straw to which it is tied. The lines then narrow their right-diagonal approach to a final twenty feet high wall of sand; in a chaotic descent nose-to-tail roped camels, necks and jaws at full stretch, kettles and pans clanking, plunge hoofs with body-jarring force into potholes created by those immediately ahead. "Sai Fachi!!"

Dearest Elle,
It's six days now since I left Agadez and twelve since we last spoke over the phone. If we were together now, here at this isolated mountain in the middle of the desert, just you and me – Such a shame you could not find it possible to fly out,
Much water, though, has by now flown under the bridge into Grovelands Lake, and I wonder if it can ever be possible for...

# NINE

It continues to smoulder, the fire ignited the previous evening by another scrumpled-up letter. The overnight blanket of a flysheet has become wet with dew – the upper corner of his sleeping bag damp, still, from a deep sadness which had extinguished the last flame of reconciliation.

Day 4 Sat 18/1 Around 9am?
Priorities. It is vitally important that I quickly establish a pattern of morning & afternoon routines – remain in full control – consolidation first & foremost – then exploration.
Therefore drive around a bit to confirm the rad leak's fixed, then climb up to the guelta & fill more containers. Hair & clothes to be shot of sand & dust…

An element of uncertainty lies hidden between the lines of a fresh page headed 'Dropped Anchor', this potential ten days or more rest-up at Madet not having been on the agenda. A minor crisis of confidence, last experienced when redundancy from Hydro Services & Installations had at a stroke terminated what had become Lanby's purpose in life – a personal mission whereby an improved quality of life was brought to those living in remote settlements. Consigned to the scrap heap, widowed, and back in UK, a habitual pint and chaser in the Salisbury then a new and wonderful relationship had nevertheless been but a treading of water until this extended *vacance* back in the region of Africa he identified with more than any other.

... but must not forget that it was Inspector Migraine's 'This time you are only a tourist' which became the catalyst for all this – has provided the opportunity to prolong the singlehanded factor with now being able to remain out of sight of land for a further two, even three weeks... making sure to guard against the spectre of (as allegedly happened to one of Moitessier's rivals in the Golden Globe yacht race) prolonged introspection to the point where one decides the time has come to just step overboard.

*Testing... Testing... two three four...*

*Now climbing the scree for a general look-around. Early to mid-morning. A watch only showing the correct time twice a day is beginning to get to me. shouldn't do, but it is.*

A daily routine is already established: pocket tape recordings of thoughts and incidents as they happen – observations of particular importance transposed to the logbook come late afternoon.

*... and the sun's been burning a hole through the back of my anorak, but now on the summit ridge there's a fresh breeze. Forty miles away, the Massif looks like the Cliffs of Dover. With binoculars I scan the desert for the slightest movement... and see swirling dust devils. But this is what I've come up for... in the trees' shadows far below I again see the gazelles. No flash of yellow this morning... no grouse flying in to soak its breast feathers at the rock pool.*

*As I make my way diagonally to a prominent point that looks like a chimney stack I see what seem to be man-made piles of rocks in the scars down Madet's west-facing side. Their black patina appearance suggest they could be ancient tombs. What did Arambey's final poem say?... Tread carefully, these rocks possess life and death... wonder if his father Harouna's grave is down there somewhere?...*

Sparrowsfart. Coffee in the office (front passenger seat of L/R garaged beneath the overhang). 'Watchman, what of the night? something something, the morning cometh...' Interrupted sleep I am no stranger to either. This time it was a loud crack, my then being conscious of a scuffing sound half-way along the side of the tent. Heart beating louder than a drum my fingers located & took a firm grip of the torch. At first the moon's glow played tricks with the tent's open flaps waving about in the breeze – a figure silhouetted against the night sky – but only my imagination for the snufflings then came to within inches of my right ear. Soon the clanking of rummagings through the rubbish pit. A torch-light investigation revealed tracks of a Desert Fox (too small for a Jackal). The loud crack, in fact, was the snapping of a dhow's mast as it rode out a squall off the coast of Zanzibar. Vivid dreams I'm having these nights – like the one where brother Harry & I, as kids, were on the rail line bridge beyond Shakespeare Cliff tunnel – next making our way to Dover Marine & being allowed on to the footplate of a Merchant Navy Class steam loco being shunted back to the sheds...

First aircraft I've seen... its high altitude roar not heard until it had passed overhead. Four vapour trails that become two. What's on THEIR lunchtime menu?

Have translated another of Arambey's poems – the one in which he describes a trapped Moufflon (or Efital as he also calls it) – its mate glaring down, filled with hatred.

A crystal clear, flat calm morning. Absolute silence... not even the buzz of a long-range fuel tanks fly...
    Strange... spooky even... listening to the playbacks of one's own voice. Intense... a little too serious...

Am again dipping into Paul Bowles' 'The Sheltering Sky', where he writes 'How many more times will you watch the full moon rise... it all seems endless'. Indeed, & given continued good health, from where might yours truly watch the next full moon's rise? And with whom? For this old so and so needs to share. Simple as that – just share, dammit!

*… and here, a short walk to the north-east, I find the desert floor dotted with trusses of yellow grass, nibbled down to their roots, plus faint hoof prints of wandering camels… Arambey's probably. Photographing artefacts that are breathtaking in their craftsmanship… flint arrow heads, green mostly… a circular flint cutting tool… and a small bone harpoon, its tip broken, unfortunately…*

In the gathering light of Day 7's crisp dawn, Lanby slid his mug of coffee on to the dashboard and tossed his woollen hat over his right shoulder on to the briefcase of documents and other valuables left open on the second row seats. A hand sweep of the steamed-up windscreen found him gazing not into loving eyes, but at the rock formations of his Land Rover's garage. Since well before daylight, further sleep had proved impossible after he'd discovered himself sat bolt upright in the sleeping bag. But how tenderly her lips had met his. How soft and reassuring had been her words of undying love. A further gulp of restorative Nescafé.

… and how have I again permitted other issues to override what I've always known – that after 32 happily married years nothing will ever part us. It was only through your vigilance at Emekachouar that I was able to press on…

*Forgive me Yvonne Lanby… I know now that you are right here… that we are making this journey together. Come, let's go for a drive, give the engine a run, keep the battery charged up, fill a couple of containers with water from Arambey's guelta.*

*Evie, look what we've found!*

... then a bit further along from the summit ridge's 'chimney stack' came the discovery of an old wine bottle wedged within a cairn of rocks. To below the level of its long neck the darkened glass was pitted & discoloured by sand & wind. Now extracted, this yellowing sheet of foolscap paper translates as a message written by a Lieutenant Vernaud (French Camel Corps?), Circa 1934 unbelievably, giving details of the patrol's ride south—westwards from Fort Pacot (Chirfa) to here. 'Il faut trouver de l'eau' the message ends. One very much hopes that he & his Meharists did not eventually die of thirst somewhere out there.

Did you feel, Lt.Vernaud, that you were being guided by Providence? That if He is to be found anywhere, then it is here in the desert? Most probably it was not your first experience of the Sahara – you had volunteered for another tour of duty in the sands, for back home on leave you'd found nothing quite as you had remembered it. So you had begun counting the days until your return to the sanctuary of silence & aridity.

Coffee in the office, Yvonne. I'm finding first light to be very special. Time together ahead of whatever this new day may bring. Rodrigo's Concerto de Aranjuez seems to be an ideal cassette as in the wing mirrors now we see a rust-red disc beginning to float above the Ténéré... which judging by the map has few landmarks between here and Bilma's Kaouar Falaise one hundred and sixty miles east from here. But no... the sun has not risen earlier over Arabia, the Red Sea, the Nile, the Tibesti Mountains... this is its first appearance... a possibly never to be forgotten day commencing right here.

Late afternoon. Corned beef hash again this evening. As the nights become milder I'll be kipping under the stars again.

Planet Madet: there's this acute awareness of one's planetary distances from Pleiades, Cassiopeia, Orion, Sirius, the Southern Cross. Emek to here was as if cruising the surface of an asteroid somewhere in the vastness of the Universe – in full view – doing what one felt to be right and heading in the direction one believed to be right. Can't do more than that. There's something very basic & pure about this desert: a traverse of some shimmering, flattened constellation of moons & stars where one navigates between life-sustaining oueds, hassis, puits & gueltas.

Single-handed yachtsmen, on the other hand, navigate from Cape to Cape with evidence of their progress lost amongst the waves. How frustrating that must be – there's nothing quite so satisfying as a rear-view mirror image of one's tyres creating a trail over virgin sands. Until wiped out by a storm they are a statement of one's intent – which I look forward to making when the day comes to leave this sheltered harbour & set course for Djanet. Emekachouar to Madet was a casual run-up to the start-line; from here on in it will quite literally be Beyond Recall.

The Call of the Sea, as they say, yet how powerful is the Call of the Desert. Or in my case this Return Call. Wind & sand collaborate in tempting one back with fresh-blown sands that half-convince the explorer inherent in every traveller that he or she is the first person ever to set foot, etc etc. And a silence which at times is filled only with the beat of one's heart & the flow of blood through one's veins. Whereas mariners can only rarely, indeed if ever, experience such complete & absolute silence. That's too bad.

Hands clasped in prayer he stands head bowed before a pile of rocks: now containing a more eulogistic message, the fifty-eight years old Camel Corp wine bottle is returned to its rightful place within the cairn.

"I name this promontory Pic Yvonne."

# TEN

On the morning of Day 11 Ed Lanby slung a light-load rucksack over one shoulder for his routine climb of the scree, ostensibly for a map and binoculars check on the best exit for his soon intended departure for Djanet. "I find this panoramic view mesmerising. Could stay here forever." 'Unlike some of the guys HSI hired in Algeria... right shit-stirrers, like Red McQuade and Wildy Wildman who hated the desert... and its mineral wealth that made possible their highly lucrative employment.' Retro Two Trucks again: mid to late 'Seventies. Countering a blustery wind he weighted the Michelin 153 with stones, reverently running his hands across the well-worn map – Hassi-Messaoud in the Grand Erg Oriental and the numerous rigs which surrounded similarly oil-rich In Amenas on the border with Libya – the three joint Hydro Services/Sonatrach sub-contracts where as one of a team of line managers he'd been responsible for '... side-ways thinking eccentrics, reclusive intellectuals and total nutters.' "Where are you now? Losers!" 'But I reckon the most volatile were those based at the artesian seismic survey sites on the Tademaït Plateau... it wasn't the geographical remoteness from In Salah or El Golea that got to their state of mind, but the sinister moods of a charcoal-black void where hidden potholes would detonate landmine-size explosions of choking red dust.' "Poxy Plateau!"

'Meanwhile', he thought, 'there may be no gazelles around but more firewood there will certainly be down there amongst the trees.'

83

'Listen well to the desert wind', Arambey wrote in his final poem, 'and if it should be...' This particular line has continued to baffle me, until this afternoon when I discovered what the 'it' IS!!

To collect more wood I'd driven round Madet's top corner – warm, clear viz, flat calm – & on down the opposite side. Plenty of dead stuff lying around, small pieces mostly & ideal for the Volcano kettle. No sign of life, but gazelle tracks everywhere. Before I could finish loading the roofrack the wind got up. Sharp gusts from out of nowhere. On approaching the top corner on my return I noticed a length of cloth that looked to have been blown half-way across the Sahara before becoming snagged by something or other. Someone's lost his Chech, I thought, but more cleaning rag would be most useful. Left the engine running & ran over to the base of the mountain. The faded black cloth was in fact caught in amongst a sand-filled pile of boulders. Without thinking I gave a tug, but it wouldn't budge. As I finally managed to yank it free a jolt like an electric shock shot through my fingers. 'No!' I yelled, horrified at what I'd done. But knew it was already too late – sensed that I may well have desecrated a grave – possibly, even, the final resting place of Harouna, Arambey's father. After pushing the cloth back in amongst what I now realised to be other prayer flags I made a hasty return, nosed the vehicle into the garage & had one very large Scotch. Idiot. How naive. How bad! Know now that I must leave Madet 'Go quickly, even before the gazelles' – that have already left.

Still no let-up in the wind. Under canvas tonight, for sure.

"What IS the bleedin' time?" '... twenty to midnight?... five past two?... has the moon now in its last quarter risen yet? Sod it, I've been up for a slash twice already...' Furious with himself, still, for his earlier transgression, Lanby lay listening to the wind and now quite different three-note dirges gusting through the roofrack: 'Ar-am-bey' ... on Adrar whatever it was I caught an 'Ef-i-tal'… hide and horns sold in the market of 'Tel-ou-ess'. "If I can find Telouess on the map… then… perhaps…"

Sleep, eventually. And around night's end the most vivid of dreams: a motoring holiday he and wife Yvonne had once made, down through Yugoslavia and on towards the Black Sea. Bulgaria. Another check-point. Why the delay? Soviet planes screaming overhead. Attacking an old farmhouse. Eastern Bloc war-games. Shells crunching into the hillside opposite, the ground beneath their car trembling to the shockwaves of a continuous bombardment.

Reverberating still. "What the… 'kingell!!" The tent is blown to the ground, entangling him in a suffocating chaos of canvas and poles and a sleeping bag which he struggles free from to blindly run barefoot for his life through acrid fog, gasping for air, until forced to pull up sharp with a twisted ankle.

When conscious of dawn's half-light and in some considerable pain Lanby hobbled back through thinning dust to be disbelieving of what he saw – the front section of his Land Rover, from the bonnet back to the front row seats – crushed flat.

# ELEVEN

A rock fall having damaged
my vehicle beyond repair

"Beyond repair... any fool can see that." Sat astride and up-turned ammo box he contemplates for a hundredth time the deep, pinkish-brown scar from where the huge boulder had tumbled square-on to the slab of rock overhang. And takes another sip of agreeably-laced coffee; two days previously and immediately after the earth tremor it had been a neat slug straight from the bottle. The combined impact of boulder and slab had burst open the second row seats doors, now stunted wings of a limestone coloured light aircraft that had nose-dived into the foot of the mountain.

With my Land Rover buried (sic)
by a rock fall I now commence
walking down this east-facing side
of the mountain to the bottom
corner – then head due south
until crossing the Agadez – Dirkou
track. God Willing.

A similar message is written in French, both ending 'Il faut trouver de l'eau' – to be dated, signed and taped to the rear door come the moment of setting out.

Forty-eight hours earlier (+/-) and when able to firmly grip a pen between trembling fingers and thumb, he'd written: ... clichés I know, for not only do I feel as if all that's happened since leaving Agadez (e.g. failure to find L'Arbre) have been but preparations for this moment, but conversely recall no matter how many nights I lay awake in that hotel bed imagining what I might do if the vehicle became immovable for whatever reason, I never really saw myself having to actually attempt a Walk Out (not to mention the worst-case scenarios I've half-prepared myself for since arriving here).

Hope to God my right ankle dosnt swell up. Hands still shaking, yet inwardly I feel calm & focused. Could be that I'm in a state of shock. Anyway, there's no drastic panic as thankfully I have provisions for a fortnight at least & if, conceivably, the Tremor has wrecked the guelta I've enough containers of water for a good ten days or more. Instinct, though, says best get moving asap...

Of the two options he saw as realistically making it to safety, initially he decided he'd walk due west, reasoning that in good visibility and with binoculars he would from the outset have his Aïr Mountains objective in view. Forty miles of reasonable terrain and sand dunes, judging from the map, to a guelta named Anakom, which appeared to be situated a couple of miles up into Takolokouzet Massif itself. But was Anakom a hamlet or an isolated, infrequently visited water hole? After long and hard deliberation, Lanby opted for the fractionally longer due south foot-slog where there'd be a far greater chance of rescue at the end of it all.

That same afternoon and all next day during which leaden clouds hung over the scene like a funereal shroud, Wanted was separated from Not Wanted and methodically listed.

Large Rucksack contains: 4 Corned Beef      3 boxes Cheese portions
                         6 Sardines          Biscuits (loose)
                         3 tins Potatoes     5 packet Soups
                         5 " Peas (small)    Tea Bags
                         2 B/Beans "         1 small tin Nescafe
                         4 tins Pineapple "  Fanta bottle (water)

Plus: Tin opener Spoons Matches Medics kit Toiliteries Salt tablets
    Torch + spare batteries Passport Vehicle Docs Logbooks/Diaries
    Mini tapes + Batteries Protractor Ruler Additional Maps Exposed
    Films Wallet u/s Watch House Keys N21 Arambey's Ex. Book
    Woollen hat Scarf Gloves Spare Shirt, Socks etc. Pens & Pencils

Strapped to top of Rucksack: lightweight Bedroll Sleeping bag Towel
                         length thin orange Rope Billy Can
                         plastic Mug

'... would have had an umbrella if it hadn't gone missing in
Niamey... must somehow manage to take the two remaining
cans of lager... firewood I anticipate finding at the end of the
first day...'

The carrying of two jerrycans of water containing approximately
four gallons apiece had from the perspective of a hotel room
been thought possible – but a dummy run back and forth
through camp whilst carrying a full rucksack quickly showed
this to be an impossibility without rest stops every fifteen to
twenty yards.

How in hell did I ever imagine myself capable of lugging two
full jerries, for in practice they almost immediately weigh a
ton! I'm in deeper shit than I thought – the water clock's
going to be ticking from the moment I start to walk. On the
plus side my right ankle, although sore still, is bandaged for
support & holding up okay... Looked at the idea of somehow
or other rigging up a Scott of the Antarctic type sledge,
dragging 2 j/cs behind me, but this would be no way come

the dunes... So that's it – only half–filled cans – weights I'll definitely be able to carry reasonable distances at a time. Am forced to sacrifice gallons of water for speed & distance – if I'm going to make it at all. Around 5 gallons therefore, plus the army canteen clipped to my belt, & the Fanta bottle. The tinned potatoes & peas also contain fluid of course.

Unroped from a contorted roofrack and set alight, the second spare wheel created high, billowing soot-black clouds which any convoy that might happen to be passing along the opposite side of the mountain would very likely spot. 'So, all of a sudden One Truck Edmund Mitchell Lanby... tomorrow... you've got nine short miles to Madet's bottom corner, then thirty-three to the Dirkou track. Only twelve miles a day.'

"... then head due south... that's right. Now to sign these two notices, today being the twenty-eighth of January." 'Umm, wonder how long it'll be before a patrol comes this way? If ever. They'll be more than welcome to the tools, spares, jerrycans of diesel, sand ladders, tent... all the food & the containers of water I cannot possibly take. Too heavy by far is that tin of Lyle's Golden Syrup, stood on a rock in all its glory.' "Out of the strong came forth sweetness... remember those words ever since I was a kid."

Mid–morning. About to leave. Third day running this blessing of an overcast sky – & relieved to say the ankle is (no, musn't tempt fate). Am reticent to leave this very special mountain of mine – gutted, too, to see what's happened to my once–indestructible Land Rover. Each day one tries to prepare oneself for the unforeseen – never ever thought I'd have to leave all this behind under such circumstances. But I'll be back, if only to re–build Yvonne's cairn which may not have withstood the Earth Tremor. I've dug a dirty great hole within which there lies hidden (until my return) – Photography gear, Cassette player, Volcano kettle, briefcase of now irrelevant literature, the last un-opened bottle of Red Label.

Chiselled off & buried also, the L/R's rear number plate, plus ignition keys.

"Okay! Let's Go!"

Lanby kicked sand over the fire's glowing ashes, taped his twin messages to the back of the Land Rover, then made final checks of his anorak, trousers and shirt pockets: pen, notebook, sunglasses, Swiss knife, binoculars, marching compass, three miles to the inch map of Madet, compact tape recorder. Goggles strapped around the top of his bush hat, tilted back for one final study of the pile of boulders that had been the entrance to Arambey's cave. A last nod and smile towards the blue plastic bowls he'd filled with water on the off-chance that the gazelles' absence was only temporary. Fashioned from rocks and stones, the Direction of Walking arrow which he felt certain could not fail to be seen by any chance arrival of a patrol or expedition. Final shoulder and waist strap adjustments to one now large and heavy rucksack.

"God give me strength and guidance. Touch. Pause. Engage… two , three, four, five, six… …. sixty-eight, sixty-nine, seventy and Down!" As his fingers slowly released their grip around the dark green plastic jerrycans' handles he focused for a moment longer on the very dusty pair of ridge-soled boots a certain beetle had once attempted to burrow beneath. "Alexander!", yelled Lanby in an explosive release of tension and relief that his right ankle was holding up. "How are things in Emekachouar?" 'Cracking up already', he thought, arching his back before again lifting clear of the ground two jerries which were initially feeling a touch lighter than on the dummy run.

"... and Down!" After a few halts and beginning to perspire he shed the backpack to locate a tin of something or other which had begun a-knocking at his spine. With the binoculars and to his left there was little to home in on across a pallid, sunless expanse of open Ténéré. Further scribbles in the pocket notepad :

At the turn-around point. Overcast still.
Anorak off & strapped to r/sack.

His motor's tyre marks showed clearly where he had on occasions driven down and then made climbs to re-fill water containers. "Guelta, have you managed to survive that minor 'quake?" A scan with the binocs saw no noticeable disruption to the sharply inclined scree. Then an unthinking glance over one shoulder broke his vow not to look back. '... but I guess there's still a remote possibility that rescue in some shape or form could this very minute be rounding the top corner... come upon the scene of destruction... see the vehicle and the messages... notice the direction arrow... look up and start waving madly to a figure stood but a couple of hundred yards away.'

Short distances, short breaks.
Musn't knacker myself. J/Cs proving quite manageable.

"Scuff scuff a-left and a-right, stepping over a lizard's snake-like trail. Scuff scuff and dusty boots, here pock-marks in the sand of .. possibly .. a Jerboa. Left Right Left Right, no gazelles or beetles or even a fly. South-east South-east, sticking close to the scree. South-east South-east, ever onwards to the bottom corner..."

Cloud now thinning.
Sun beginning to break through.

With plus or minus twice times one thousand seven hundred & sixty yards under his belt he makes for the segmented shade of what he sees to have originally been one quite gigantic boulder. Without even attempting to remove his pack he lays back against a conveniently angled one hundred million years old chunk of geological history – knees up, head resting on crossed arms which feel close to being parted from their sockets. Aching eyes stare at frayed edges of dust-caked slacks. Slowly and with exaggerated care he places both sunglasses and hat to one side before raising his sweat-stained face to an unexpected flow of cool air.

> Hardly a cloud in the sky now.
> La chaleur. Ca commence.
> Gone midday surely. Sun revealing
> low dunes – out there!
> Not hungry, but ravenous for a
> bar of chocolate.

Another swig of luke-warm water. 'Could be six or seven miles still to go… never get there in daylight at this rate. Damn good job I brought the gloves.' "Just relax old mate… give the mitts a break and try to take things as they come."

"… what's in these jerries?… Golden bleedin Syrup? And Down!"

> Hardly a breath of wind. Baking
> hot. Still hugging the scree. Compact
> sand with mini dunes here & there.

Lanby angled the bush hat's rim across his right eye then, as if waiting for someone else to catch him up, hesitated as he leant forward for the next Hold and Lift. It had taken the full distance of his first stint of the afternoon for the feet to regain their natural shuffling, scuffling stride. "Crouch…". Further hesitation for a self-congratulatory nod of the head for having somehow resurrected sufficient will-power to move on. 'Could so easily have called it a day back there… gone to sleep in that beautiful shade.' "And Lift two three four…" He regretted, now, after so short a distance covered, having chosen to unfold the Michelin 153. 'At this rate of progress I'll never achieve my anticipated twelve miles a day… could take five days to reach the track. Five gallons of water… forty long miles… and after just a morning I've had to re-fill the canteen.' "Don't even think about it!" The map had again brought to light the question to which there was no answer – had failed to allay increasing doubts that a single black line between the Aïr Mountains and Dirkou represented a track in regular use. Moussa's reminiscences had suggested that most days vehicles set off from Agadez on the two-day crossing, but failed to mention the latest restrictions – if in retirement he was aware of them even. 'If Migraine was not telling forbidden routes porky-pies, and whether or not Fall Arnaud's marker posts are still standing, the Dirkou track might at this moment in time be little more than partially visible sets of sand-filled tramlines. I'd considered this aspect when deciding to walk south, not west, from Madet, but it's a scenario that's reared its ugly head again. Need to just keep reminding myself that on the morning before leaving Emekachouar I definitely spotted a convoy that had to have been making for Dirkou. And or Bilma.' "So forget it!"

'Although forget I cannot and forget I must not, the clear responsibility which is mine regarding old Arambey's anthology. When found in the cave I tended to think that it had not been left behind purely by accident, the final poem seeming to confirm this to have been the case… je vous dit Adieu mon ami… yet even though the last verse now suggests that he may have ridden off for a rendezvous with destiny, his writings do not automatically become my possession.' Lanby halted and knelt in prayer, a weight far, far greater than that of the rucksack stood upright in the sand now lifted from his shoulders: without any shadow of doubt a convoy would appear and transport him to safety – if not directly to Agadez then eastwards to Dirkou – it didn't matter in the slightest – then somehow or other a way would be found whereby the exercise book could be returned to its rightful owner. '… and should I be too late, then to his family in Iferouane.' He removed the poly-bag protective cover and exposed its graph-lined pages to the same cloudless sky and glinting sunlight under which he imagined many of the poems would have been composed. Circling the backpack and jerrycans, book in hand, Lanby read a sense of duty and a re-fortification of purpose into every line, before once again loading up and walking on, reflecting further on the part he himself had had to play in his guide and translator's later years. The now-recognizable parity, also, between 'On Adrar Tamaskaouene… hunting for Moufflon… a falcon's shadow passed over my head…' and 'On Adrar Madet… hunting for firewood… the earth trembled beneath my feet…' "Having made his escape from Agadez he arrived an hour too late, yet if he'd reached Adrar Madet even a decade ago he'd have still been too early for… for… what am I trying to say? Er, not early enough by far, to explore that solitary and magnificent mountain…. to in its peaceful solitude attempt to understand the real Edmund Mitchell… the piecing together of a jigsaw which… which trudging across the desert with a twisted ankle whilst slowly going round the twist will hopefully prove not to be the final piece. Or something."

Late afternoon. Flat calm. Cloudless still. Absolutely all in. Painful hands, limbs, knees, shoulders – twinges over the last stretch have resulted in my right ankle swelling up a bit. No ticker problems,Thank God.Been here about half an hour. Guesstimate my position to be a couple of miles short of the bottom corner.

Cracking open the second v.warm Heineken.

"Medaille D'Or Paris Eighteen seventy-five, it reads. Diplome D'Honneur Amsterdam Eighteen eighty-three. Vent au Niger. Serve cool, it says in English. Ha! Keep your country a clean place. Don't litter. Sante!!"

There's enough wood lying around for a fire. Must eat something. Corned beef, spuds and peas.

Cannot possibly continue lugging all this gear under a blazing hot sun.

Suicidal.

# TWELVE

A whiff of smoke awakens him; the pleasant aroma forever to be associated with Dvorak, Tchaikovsky, snifters and cordon-bleu tin-opening below ridge summit. "Wind's re-ignited the embers" he mutters to himself, eyes shut tight still, mind and body more rested following his decision to await sunset before making a dash for it.

Resignedly he parts both eyelids to the canopy of shrubs crashed out under a while earlier, first casting an abortive glance at his left wrist then checking the sun's position in a part-clouded sky. 'Hour or two? Anyway, managed to get a decent kip.'

At first light he had completed the trek to Madet's southern-most point, there to discover sets of vehicle tracks. Four motors, their sand-blown tyre marks leaving him uncertain if the convoy had driven in from the east then headed off in a south-westerly direction, or if in fact the opposite had been the case. Evidence of a *mechoui* – the pit, ashes, a carcass, Dorcas horns. Plus one large and very empty plastic Coca Cola bottle, complete with screw top. In the process of transferring jerrycan water to the Fanta and Coke bottles, carelessly spilt drops were as those of his very own blood quickly soaked up by thirsty gravel.

Dawn's fresh northerly tail-wind had helped make the last couple of mile's hike less exhausting than expected – a telling factor when mid-morning on this second day of his attempted Walk Out he'd written … an idea I've been toying with since yesterday afternoon – 33 miles to the Dirkou track, with no shade whatsoever here on in, means that if I'm to survive at all I'm going to have to walk during the cool of night (by starlight, only a crescent moon rising late now), & rest up throughout the heat of the day. The concept of what he dubbed a Lightweight Dash had immediately lifted his spirits. To the Not Wanted pile of spare clothing, sardines, packet soups and bed roll was added the billy can, after a last hot meal, some sleep and final preparations.

Bottom Corner Adrar Madet Wednesday the Twenty-ninth of January. Sun now beginning to dip. Ahead and southwards, according to the map, there'll be four miles of level terrain, twelve miles of north-east to south-west linear dunes, then a final seventeen of flat, featureless desert. Should I not make it, then whoever, would you kindly ensure that the exercise book of poetry reaches its owner, Arambey of Iferouane. God grant I make it to the track.

There being no positive landmarks he held the compass in front of his waist and orientated on to the required one hundred & eighty degrees heading. Once locked on to a particular hump on the immediate horizon he readjusted the rucksack's position on his back, donned gloves, hat and sunglasses, grabbed the pair of now marginally less heavy jerrycans and resumed his metronomic pace – again vowing not to look back at a mountain he had not only come to know well, but which in return he believed now knew him also; better even than he understood himself.

"This is more like it… and Down!. Phew!… sweating like mad… but two hundred yards at least in one go."

*Hard ground. Promising start. Aches and pains of yesterday dissipating... for the moment anyway.*

Re-orientation on the next mound. Compass and tape recorder slid back into anorak pockets. Lips-moistening swig from the canteen. Hat tugged down against a scarlet sun's oblique, departing rays. "... Pause... Engage... two three four..."

He'd progressed what he imagined to be one and a half to two miles when, like Pathfinder vapour trails joining a coordinated angle of attack, four sets of vehicle tracks swept in from behind his right shoulder to join his own due south trajectory. Holding that line still as night began to fall.

*Walking parallel now with the convoy's eight inter-winding tyre ruts across this flat plain. Not recent tracks, but sufficient incentive to picture their base camp just up ahead.*

*Wind now gusting from the north-east. Am willing these vehicle tracks to hold one-eighty on through the dunes, which in semi-darkness can be seen in the distance... meaning I wont have to keep stopping to check my compass direction every few minutes.*

To double-check the batteries he stopped to flash a beam of torchlight across the conjoined set of tracks at his feet. Then between intakes of now cooler air as he walked on, whispered "Lull before the storm", all too aware that before very long the crust of firm earth over which his boots slid with ease would swiftly turn into a full-on assault course – ridges of alternating soft and firmish sands extending southwards for a dozen or so miles – an abrupt end to his comfort zone of rhythmic stride, pause for breather, message recorded, slug of water, gloves back on again routine that was seeing him make steady progress.

"Bad enough not knowing the hour of day, let alone the night." 'Wasn't all that far away from here', he reflected whilst halting to relieve himself, '... a fortnight ago, when the watch died an untimely death... maybe ten to fifteen miles south-west from here on the drive up from Emek.' He pressed on, treading the convoy's tracks which in emerging starlight could now be seen closing on the blacker than night barriers of transverse dunes. 'If I recall correctly, the sun sets in these parts around six o'clock, then at possibly two miles an hour with nigh-on four miles covered, the time has to be getting on for eight... means the waning crescent moon cannot be expected to rise above the eastern horizon for another two and a half to three hours... if I've got that right. Not that its very welcome sight and glow will be all that beneficial... additionally beneficial I should perhaps say... for it is quite amazing how rapidly one's eyes adjust to a starlit night such as this.'

A short distance into the dune's border edge pattern of low, rolling hillocks and not altogether to his surprise having driven through this same *erg,* albeit more to the west, the four sets of increasingly faint tyre treads cut across to the right in order to penetrate a fault in the first formidable ridge at its shallowest angle. After intense deliberation, the fear being that such meanderings from one gap to the next would add considerable time and distance to his determined aims, Lanby chose to stick with the tracks; for a short while at least. But having entered a further *ghassi* the Pathfinders, as if suddenly diverted to pinpoint an alternative target, disappeared into the gloom, south-westwards again, in the direction of Areschima Sud. Stunned by the very abruptness with which this umbilical, virtually tactile link with the outside world had been severed he stood rooted to the spot, peering forlornly into a darkness where he might yet

have come upon a patrol's base camp situated less than...
"Merde!!"

Using a pencil he marked his estimated position on the large scale map and dropped the torch back into its anorak slot, compass and self now aligned with a particular star which seemed to bob up and down atop the next flat-topped incline. His deep drawl betrayed little of an escalation of concern that had risen a notch or two: *Ahead now, according to the map, more of what I became familiar with on the drive from Areschima to Madet... corridors of dunes at most twenty to thirty feet high. Where I am situated is just an extension of that same system. Except, of course, I cannot now waste precious energy trying to locate faults in the lines. At night, not an option. Nothing for it but to head in as straight a line as possible over whatever comes up. I give thanks that the ankle is now one hundred percent okay again.*

The valleys separating each line had yet to narrow, but every dune descent was proving to be as tiring as the sharpish struggle to the next crest where to pause for breath, take a swig of water, jot something in the notebook, and from time to time unlace the boots to jettison "... half the sodding Sahara!" When stationary he yanked his anorak's hood over a sweaty shirt collar and woollen hat to counter the cold north-easter. Visibility remaining clear; a cast of thousands upon thousands, with the crescent moon yet to appear on stage. All-important sightings of the Southern Cross. Then a sharp kick in the guts with a belated realization that the combined climbs and descents of dune after dune would mean there'd be a greater distance to cover than the straight line twelve miles ruler measurement on the map.

*… how obvious was that? Tiring fast. Must call a halt soon. Waves of sand. How did Moitessier put it?… one forgets oneself, forgets everything, seeing only the ply of the boat with the sea. Just one more line, then need to get some food down me.*

A well-practised crab-like manoeuvre, balanced by adept handling of the two half-filled jerrycans of water took him to the bottom – an unstable descent to dark, compacted ground, reminiscent of his years spent 'down pit' as a Bevin Boy when called up towards the end of the Second World War to work at the Cannok Chase coalfield in Staffordshire. Hard yet good years which amongst other things had cured his childhood fear of the dark. 'Eventually became a Tadgerman', he smiled to himself, 'drilling holes in the coalface… and they called me Tadger Lanby, should I happen to be so lucky.'


The motionless air is but a few degrees above freezing. Now risen clear of the horizon the sun's warmth has yet to penetrate the back of his anorak – the same faded blue and worse for wear anorak he'd pulled over his shoulders as the dust had settled over the crumpled Land Rover. Just four days ago, when he'd found himself introduced to someone he'd never before met, who coped with the traumas immediately following a minor earthquake by partaking the role of a casual observer totally detached from over-hasty, ill-conceived decisions.

This same someone sat close to the top of a high dune distancing himself even more from reality – dangerously so – his tried and earth tremor tested method of survival. Whose blistered fingers make a perfunctory attempt to comb straight a determinedly unruly beard, then dab at flaked skin around his mouth. Whose eyes heavy with fatigue and in their own time make their way back down deep boot-holes to the rippled floor of a narrow gulley in partial shadow, to the spot where a call to nature had been answered, then back across to where the footprints had separated from some vagrant's belongings – sleeping bag, backpack, bush hat, gloves – the avalanche-razed slope above telling its very own story of his exhausted arrival at some unearthly hour of the night. An Ed Lanby sat wondering who in his right mind would have set off on foot across so punishing and imprisoning waves of sand – from that grey mound of a mountain still visible seven or eight miles away. Heading due south, meaning a further seven of eight miles of dunes and seventeen of flat terrain on top of that before achieving the first stage of his aim. A 'Lightweight Dash' which now finds him down to a maximum four gallons of water, with no alternative whatsoever but to battle on through the unremitting heat of a day that has begun cloudless and crystal clear.

"Unless!" As his aching shoulders finally receive *le soleil's* undivided attention Lanby pencils a cross marking his probable position, studies the map once more, then cracks a lip in shouting "Yes!"

> Tin of pineapple for breakfast. Am reticent to tape record the seriousness of my situation. It's now all or nothing. No way can I stick to due south. Map shows the dunes to peter out 4 or 5 miles SW from where I believe myself to be, so am going for it – SW along (not over) dune lines to flatter ground, then SSE to the Dirkou track. Bit further to walk, but have no option⋯ .

He felt a surge of adrenalin when gingerly topping-up the canteen and soft drinks bottles, decanting what water remained into one jerrycan – at a little over half full able to fairly effortlessly be transferred from one hand to the other when necessary. 'Dunes shift, but I'm pinning my hopes on this IGN map remaining sufficiently accurate twenty years on.' "Orientating on to two hundred and twenty... here we go!"

With the sun over his left shoulder and before getting into his stride along a firm-based gulley he looked back, to see the empty jerrycan placed near the top of the high dune toppled by the arrival of a fresh, remaining north-easterly, breeze.

*Feel like a weather vane. Listening to what its saying, Arambey. Toute a droit.*

A subtle shift in wind direction coincided with formations of scattered cloud, affording brief respites of shade and a quickening of pace as with the sun reaching its zenith Lanby noticed the dunes on his left to appreciably decrease in height – the overlapping *ghassis* and broadening corridors slogged along for his estimated four or five miles gradually fanning out to become a shimmering void.

Open desert at last!
But what a Catch-22
What a ham-fisted bastard.

After much rummaging he located the tin-opener, then through parched lips savoured every drop of a green and delicious fluid before devouring the can of peas from the palm of his hand. The jerrycan and rucksack formed an effective windbreak. Anorak over head he sought oblivion from the torrid morning's Catch-22 of 'sweating buckets' countered by 'drinking gallons' – and above all try to forget forever that this ham-fisted so-&-so had let slip the Fanta bottle to watch with horror as dark splodges marked its tumbling sand-slide to the base of the dune he'd climbed for a binoculars view of what lay ahead. Yet even when he'd have opted for any one of his recent nightmares, sleep proved elusive – until utter exhaustion crept in through a side-entrance.

Sundown. Thirtieth of January. A Thursday if I'm not mistaken. Am now approximately fifteen miles south-west from Adrar Madet. Intend marching for as long as I am physically capable. Il faut trouver la piste.

Lanby satisfied himself that he was sufficiently clear of the sand sea, pencilled his rough position on the large-scale map, then orientated on to the new heading of one hundred and fifty degrees. "The day I arrive back in England will be a Thursday" he shouted at the ground, endeavouring to pretend they were not HIS knees and shoulders rebelling furiously at yet again having to bear the weight of a cumbersome rucksack – were someone ELSE'S pain-wracked hands being forced into gloves that would take turns in carrying the jerrycan. "Here in my wallet", he grimaced as his left foot reluctantly took the initial step, "... there's a Freedom Pass that will take me down the escalators to a Piccadilly Line train... rush hour through Town... Leicester Square, Covent Garden, Holborn. And Down! Phew! Sod this for a lark... and Lift!" 'So who are all these people and where are they going?... he could be some office manager from Southgate... she'll very likely be getting off at Turnpike Lane... and this scruff with a rucksack? Oh, he's recently managed to walk out of the Sahara Desert. Pull the other one. God, what wouldn't I do to be on a tube train right this minute.' He closed his eyes. "Our Father who art in Heaven, grant that I make it back home again. And Rest!"

Dusk. Making reasonable progress. Cool. Flat calm now. High whispy cloud.

Before walking on he remained motionless for many minutes, deeply inhaling an intoicatingly pure air, listening intently to an all-pervading silence, inviting the strengths felt present within his surroundings to re-energize those senses of an

104

increasingly fatigued self. His natural rhythm then returned and he became mindful, as more noisily than ever his boots scuffed loose surfaces, of the dark plain he'd crossed when setting out from Bottom Corner. 'Little over twenty-four hours ago… stroll on, I've only been averaging about three-quaters of a mile an hour. This sunset there were eighteen or thereabouts to go… have possibly covered four since then… so on this flat terrain and if I can up the average to two miles an hour… a very big ask.' "Another break."

But as Lanby entered the night so a curtain of haze drifted across the constellations of Winter: with no Southern Cross or other stars clearly visible he began to find the imperative of time-consuming torch and compass orientation halts irksome. Thought he was hallucinating when haze-obscured triple shooting stars created a brief fireworks display across the south-eastern skyline.

Thus far he has managed to keep his vivid imagination in check regarding the Sword of Damocles scenarios of mental exhaustion, physical injury, serious illness, sandstorms, zero visibility, critical shortage of water, total disorientation with its attendant fate – the numerous 'what ifs' that could at any moment pull him up sharp in his tracks. Yet it is the very next routine halt for a guzzle and breather which proves to be the last straw after a gruelling day and now ominously dark night. "Merde!" he yells, bent double, his full weight upon the jerrycan as intuition issues a warning that the weather might be about to clamp down. Patiently he allows his be-numbed brain time to transmit the necessary instructions to raptor-clawed fingers stubbornly refusing to loosen their grip on the green plastic *bidon's* handle. When finally upright again he thrusts a hand into the torch compartment of his anorak. Empty. The other pockets?: map, tape recorder, notebook, compass… "Where the fuck is it?… can't have fallen out. When did I last use the torch? Must have left it lying on the ground at the last stop, or if not used, then the stop before that even. Stay calm. Stay calm. What to do. What to do. Drop everything and retrace my footprints in the sand. It's pitch dark. Can't be more than a few hundred yards. No! Crash out right here… flat as a pancake but as good a place as any. Go back for it in the morning. Idiot! Beginning to feel I'm done for. Must get some food down me."

Deep in his sleeping bag he presses the record button of a rectangular shape identical to that of the pocket Bible presented to him on the occasion of his Confirmation at St. Andrew's Parish Curch, Enfield Town. Forgive me, Dearest Elle, for all the hurt that I have caused. It's Eddie… Mitch… seem to have got myself in a bit of a fix. Feel to be on the far side of the moon. Yes, I've had a drink… stashed away a large snifter so as to celebrate my rescue in style… which now looks to be unlikely. This is what you find. Just want you to know, Eleanor, that should I fail to reach the Dirkou track… want you to believe me when I say that from that very first evening when we were introduced to one-another… what I mean is that I pray we might yet be together again… very soon… take a stroll around Grovelands Park… just as we always did, before…

# THIRTEEN

Wham! His whole being shudders to a huge, tension-exploding wave. Knocking him on to his side. Then further ebbing and flowing of the Indian Ocean's tidal surge, keeping perfect time with deep inhalations and exhalations – Shreee… Shraaa… Shreee… Shraaa… – warm tropical waters advancing and receding Shreee… Shra… Bham!! The second hit, twice as powerful as the first, contorts his haggard, prostrate form into a steel-tight coil. No dream, the stench of the towel covering his face confirms that, but he double-checks – that indeed he is still alive – by flexing a thumb to the pulsations of a wrist lodged beneath his chin. He shoves his feet to the bottom of the sleeping bag '… pair of socks down there somewhere.' Whinces as his efforts re-open the cracked top lip. 'Bugger-all viz… had a feeling that thick brume would descend overnight… meaning it won't be a scorcher like yesterday.' First remembering to check for hidden scorpions he laces his boots, the decision already made not to squander priceless time, energy and above all water re-tracing sand-blown footprints in search of a senior moment torch left lying somewhere back there behind a dense curtain of fog.

Fri 31/1 Guesstimate 08.00 Approx 10 or 11 miles NW of the track.
Canteen & both plastic bottles re–filled, leaving a gallon or so in the j/can.
Mercifully a calm, cool morning, the sun totally hidden by thick brume. But it has been an interminable night

of doubts & fears – dreading another Ténéré Tree-like vent de sable – vowing that should I reach safety I will mend my ways once & for all. Arambey described how in remote areas he felt to be in company with Allah – as this morning I awoke feeling completely at one with myself & in His Presence. Relaxed. Trusting. Accepting that this is the way things are meant to be – doing what I feel to be right, heading in the direction I believe to be right. Can do no more than that. 'Place your Trust in God' dear old Grandma Lanby used to say. That I do.

After half a dozen brief pauses across flat, firm sands Lanby unexpectedly found himself entering an area of crescent moon *seif* dunes '... in all probability started a few years ago by the carcass of some unfortunate gazelle.' He climbed a higher transverse dune from where, in the uniform haze-diffused light of the *ghassi* below, it took him some moments to realise that his tired eyes were gazing down upon series of fresh tracks. Camel hoof tracks. Heading west. He looks to his right, simultaneously throwing the jerrycan to the ground.

When, the previous evening, an unbalanced load within their inherited *azalai* resulted in a broken shoulder blade, they'd turned the stricken camel's head in the direction of Mecca, slit its throat, and in their late father's memory revelled in the rare opportunity of being able to gorge themselves on as much fresh, boiled meat as they could stomach. Stomachs conditioned week in, week out, to an unchanging diet of millet pap. Now, the morning after, doubled-up with indigestion and hastening after elder brother Agaly riding on ahead, Boubaka pulls up sharp. Momentarilly having lost sight of their lines as they entered the isolated dune formation, it is in disbelief that he suddenly spots a figure hurl his backpack to one side, wave frantically in the direction of the disappearing caravan, then set off in pursuit – only to trip and tumble over and over down the dune's shallow incline.

Laying there, still. Motionless. "M'sieur! ça va M'sieur? Lafiya? M'sieur!!"

It was not until gone midday that the brume slowly unveiled its impersonation of a full moon. In the realization that they must have drifted some way off course and with an ever-watchful eye on the sick person slumped across his belongings atop a lightly laden camel towards the rear of their salt caravan, the teenagers nudged their lead camels' noses towards the hazy sun in an adjustment to the direction they'd taken soon after leaving Fachi, three days ago, the tiny oasis of lower grade *salines* where earlier and on completion of the first stage of the four hundred miles trek from Bilma back to Agadez, Tazrine and his sons had set up camp beneath palm trees to rest, take on water and retrieve the bales of *alemoz* left in safe keeping on the outward journey. And buy more bottles of mixture from the Tibbu's general store, for pain and prolonged fits of coughing had often left Tazrine scarcely able to walk. So it was, that on the morning of their intended continuation westwards through the Erg, Agaly and Boubaka had found it impossible to rouse their father for his first glass of chai. And it had therefore transpired, that following Tazrine bin Warariz's burial in Fachi's *caravaniers'* cemetery and the sale of half the herd, his sons chose not to join other groups, proudly setting off in the rough direction of Aïr with ten camels apiece packed with bollard-shaped *kantus* of far superior salt from Kalala.

They had taken care not to part with their father's small brass camel's bell. Without slowing his line and with a loud thump, Agaly leapt bare foot to the ground. Dates in pocket and with an enamel mug of water from one of their two remaining half-empty goatskins, he strode in warm sunshine now alongside the camel on which the man they had that morning rescued continued to drowse, rocking back and forth, saved only from crashing to earth by his gloved hands' clinging-on-tight to the twin straw bales' cross-connecting ropes. "Sannu! Sannu M'sieur Edhey" When he came to, *le turist* met at Amzeguer who had generously given their father a *cadeau* of fifty thousand CFA before driving on in his *mota,* was handed up further food and drink. The dates were transferred to an anorak pocket. Once every final drop had been savoured he gratefully passed the mug back down to a youth whose face he found vaguely familiar. "Merci. Ou sommes nous? Ou est Greboun?" After some hesitation Agaly replied "Tafagag… Labara… quelle direction Monsieur?" As the greybeard they'd believed to be well aware of their exact position now stared back with a blank expression on his face, oblivious to the question as to which direction the Tree and its Wells might lie, the young Targui scurried back to the head of the camel train, close to tears.

Lanby sat up straight, rolled his shoulders and gave his bush hat a sharp downward tug. Then another, in order to comprehend why he was seeing what he saw. 'This has to be some weird sort of dream, for the plan was to take four camels… now there are about twenty of the sodding things. Why such a large caravan, loaded with so many sacks of provisions simply for a few day's ride up and around Adrar Greboun? At least I can see one of them over there, tied to the side of a… why does everyone call them camels? . . bleedin' dromedaries aren't they… but where's that second jerrycan of mine?' Astride a saddle of hump and sacking whilst grasping hold of his rucksack and the cross-connecting ropes for dear life, he suddenly felt himself sent again tumbling into a dark abyss – then back into blinding sunlight where his loose cannon of a mind continued to fire irrational, scrambled thoughts regarding the inexplicable situation he found himself to be in. 'Those two lads up front… don't recall it being necessary to hire additional help.' "Arambey! Where are you old mate?" Again startled by his cries, yet tacitly agreeing that the man found staggering through the dunes was perhaps enduring another fever-driven outburst, the young brothers resumed their anxious questionings as to where they were, the amount of water remaining in the two *guerbas,* together with the plight of someone they now considered it their responsibility to get to Agadez hospital as soon as possible. Leaving them shuddering with fright, for there was no immediate sign of Labara coming up on the horizon. Neither had they encountered another salt caravan since leaving Fachi.

When Agaly ventured back down his line with another mug of water, M'sieur Edhey was wide awake and pointing to his right. Pointing towards open desert. "Caught up with us at last. Nothing more to worry about. Over there… look… that's my friend Arambey, who knows this area like the back of his hand."

"S'il vous plaît?"

"There… in the blue and black robes and green chech… riding his favourite white mehari. Fifty yards away. Are you blind?"

"Errr… il y a ne rien."

"I've just checked our compass heading my lad. We've made good progress since heading out of Iferouane yesterday morning. As I'm sure you know, the mountain where we'll spend a few days, called Adrar Greboun, is the highest in Niger. Should be visible any time, now the fog's cleared."

"Excusez-moi M'sieur, mais…"

"What's that? Yes, you are perfectly correct… Arambey's ridden ahead… swung south. He's beckoning for us to keep up. Tell your friend to alter course. Gauche. Tell him… we've got to keep that rider in sight as he knows the shortest route. When we make camp tonight he'll come over to join us for chai. Can't wait for his reaction when I hand him his exercise book. Go on, tell him!… gauche for heavens sake!"

"D'accord M'sieur." Agaly ran to assist in hauling their lines to the left, agreeing with Boubaka that it would be best to do as instructed by the man from *Ingila* who seemed to know where they were – a commanding voice, similar to that of their late father – but whose camel-riding guide named Arambey remained invisible to their weary eyes.

* * *

"Ah, a knock on the door. Oui, c'est ma valise. Merci beaucoup. C'est pour vous.''

'Too late, meant to ask where they've hidden the ashtray. Bit of a bummer, reception telling us they need to hang on to our passports until morning. Feel naked without it. Wish those Swiss couples didn't make such a racket deciding which room is whose. Now, let's see… water running from both taps… and yes, here it is. This will be my second, if not third ciggy in Africa. No opening of duty frees, just yet.'

Hotel. Agadez. Friday 31st January.
Here! A small miracle. Arrived nervous as a kitten,

112

half expecting Edmund to have already returned from Lake Chad. With some woman on his arm, if I'm honest. Reception showed me M.Lanby's reservation, this coming Monday 3rd of February.

Not an enormous room, but tidy & clean. Large mattress. Small wardrobe, but it'll do. The evening meal is from seven o'clock, so have a couple of hours to get organized. Decide what to wear.

We all agreed how fortunate we were to have got that flight from Niamey to here. Something about this runway having been closed for some months and that it was only because some government officials needed to be in Agadez in a hurry that we are here now. Would otherwise have meant a six hundred mile journey overland. Wonder if they'll have fish on the menu?

'Goodness, they know the barman's name already. Popular place, but apart from the Swiss couples I can't see any other… Oh come on Amadou, my turn next.'

"Oui. Gin et tonic Madame… avec glace?"

"Non merci."

'So glad I didn't change', Eleanor Staunton thought with a concealed sigh of relief, having decided for the first evening to stick with the Deborah Kerr-on-Safari khaki skirt outfit and sensible shoes. Nervously, she slid on to a stool that appeared as if from nowhere, avoiding eye contact with the owner of slim black fingers proffering a cigarette lighter over her shoulder. Drink finally in hand she exhaled with unintentional haste and stared at her 'not a pretty sight' self in the bar's lengthy mirror. 'Cheers, and remember what you were told… act as though you've lived here all your life.' A casual glance at the framed photograph of the Head of State, resplendent in military uniform, peering down from on high. Attention then shifting to the collection of once colourfully labelled liqueurs clogging the mirror's shelf. 'It's like being at the cinema – fascinating, trying to match voices propping up the bar with the line-up of faces on the silver screen opposite. Those three were on the plane, and he…'

"Excusez-moi, Amadou… est-ce-que… err… do you by any chance know of a gentleman named Hamouri ?"

* * *

Upon departing the Kaouar falaise and returning westwards through the Bilma Grand Erg they had thought only of meeting up again with elder brother Bazo and of joining him in cadging gifts from visitors to Agadez market. Devastated by Tazrine's death and burial at Fachi the teenagers had chosen to independently continue across the Ténéré as a demonstration of their intention to follow family tradition and be seen as *madugus* in their own right – proudly re-entering their home village of Marandet with a caravan of fine Bilma salt in tribute to their late father. Overnight almost, sixteen and seventeen year olds become men, unaware of a change in mannerisms as they sat huddled close to their fire with blankets clutched about their necks like true *caravaniers,* Agaly and Boubaka waited patiently for the sun to rise into a clear sky above the flat and desolate expanse now behind them. Like veteran *madugus* they thoughtfully poked away at the crimson embers, flipping the lids of their chaipots in mock astonishment at the time it took them to come to the boil, ever alert to the muffled groans and sighs of their cud-chewing herd – nineteen camels now after an *alum* disovered to have a fractured shoulder was slaughtered. And, unconsciously perpetuating the cavalier attitude of some leaders of salt caravans, they'd carelessly run out of water.

It had been well after dark when they'd eventually unloaded, fed the animals, then used much of their remaining firewood to boil more fresh meat; Edhey's green plastic *bidon* raided this morning now virtually empty and laying on its side in the sand. With uncertainty they awaited his reaction, loath after their experience at Fachi to try to rouse him in case there was no response, for having opened a can of food soon after halting for the night he had straightway and with difficulty crawled utterly exhausted into his sack. But as the small teapots began to bubble and spit so *le turist d'Ingila* awoke, tied his boot laces, hauled his anorak over both shoulders and came across to the fire, accidently kicking the jerrycan as he did so.

"Babu ruwa, Monsieur."

"So I see." Lanby shook his head in scarce surprise and walked back to the rucksack, returning with his two large, three-quarters full soft drink bottles of water.

"Kai!!"

When a glass of chai was passed to him Lanby sat contemplating the flickering flames, remembering little since making a diary entry the morning after losing the torch.

They had not expected their friend's 'tempest of the head' to be cured without *magani,* their father having warned them of the terrible things that happened to those who lost their way in the desert. Tazrine's wise words they had rarely heeded, but come dawn and in the hope of reaching Amzegeur and then Agadez hospital as quickly as possible – the mountains were clear to be seen and perhaps less than a day's ride away – the brothers had drawn circles in the sand around each palm frond-wrapped load as a safeguard, in traditionally recognised fashion, until such time as they were able to return and retrieve their temporarily abandoned pillars of salt.

I give thanks this morning, also to these salt caravan lads I am with, for being alive, having been to hell and back... left with only faint recollections of what happened yesterday... er... that's right... yesterday. Still got a severe headache and am taking paracetamol. The mountains are now in sight and very shortly Boubaka, Agaly and I will be making a dash for it, being extremely low on water. They couldn't believe it when I opened the last tins of pineapple to share before setting out. God grant we reach safety.

First negotiating a zig-zag path between *seif* dunes, the camels then trod their own rapidly depleting shadows out and across a further spirit-level *reg* of firm, orange sands. "Alhamdulillah" his companions were heard to mutter to themselves as the three rode alongside one-another at the head of an unladen caravan – save personal belongings, pots and pans, slivers of firewood and the remaining half-bale of fodder. But with now only makeshift and unsupported saddles of blankets, sacking and sleeping bag it was found easier to walk for much of the time. At each pause to rest Lanby compared the map with a gradually changing outline of grey-blue mountains an indeterminate way away and possibly a full day's march still. Sticking to his compass heading of west-south-west they pressed on, soon to enter corridors of transverse dunes. 'What nutcase drove alone across such remote terrain?' Lanby had questioned when a while back his boots scuffed the barely visible tramlines of a vehicle's tracks – only to realise that in all probability their position was south of the star dune Areschima Sud – likewise that the tracks they'd crossed were those made by his very own Land Rover on the drive up from Emekachouar to Madet.

"Lafiya?... ça va, Edhey?"

"Oui, ça va... mais..."

Their prayers were answered when towards late afternoon and close to total exhaustion they found themselves approaching a small army of camels and riders – a Bilma-bound *azalai* setting out from Oued Tafidet whose *madugu,* learning of his friend Tazrine's passing and immediately realising how critical things were, called a halt and made camp there and then.

Come morning Agaly, Boubaka and Lanby bade farewell, then with food and water sufficient for the completion of their journey finally entered the Aïr along a deep-worn trail which brought them to the foothills village of Tazizilet. And beyond.

# FOURTEEN

"Babu ruwa" the silversmith whispered to himself as with a roar reminiscent of rain-charged storms that once thundered and echoed through the mountains, a chartered Boeing 737 ferrying vital supplies swept low over a sleeping Agadez and its shanty town of drought-striken refugees. Stood at the rear entrance of his modest mud-brick house he watched the plane until lost from sight, then clicked his tongue a few times. In the semi-darkness of the open enclosure his horse reacted with a sharp tug on its rope tether. Hamouri shook his head, pacing up and down, before returning to bed; the violent Tuareg uprising and government reprisals were moving ever closer, but for the moment at least the pockets of his *gandoura* carried many old and valuable Crosses. After making wife Tinna's chai he would see to Amadou's request.

Hotel de l'Air
Agadez
Saturday 1st February

Dear Janice,

I have arrived! A long haul, mostly uneventful, with the surprise bonus of reaching here a little earlier than expected. 'You Know Who' has yet to show up – in two day's time, according to hotel reception who were informed by Edmund that he was visiting Lake Chad.

Please thank Neil (& Philip) for their invaluable advice (first time in Africa, alone, etc) that when in public I should behave like an ex-pat who's been here years. Worked a treat in the hotel bar last evening, followed by an enjoyable evening meal with two charming Swiss couples.

Must confess I'm extremely apprehensive as to how things will go on Monday, but still have no doubts in my mind whatsoever that what I'm doing is right. Right for us both, hopefully & most importantly.

Having a late breakfast whilst writing this, as a member of staff has kindly said he'll make sure my letter catches this morning's post.

Love to you both

"Still don't care much for these dark blue curtains. So dingy in here." Eleanor Staunton reiterated her first impressions of the restaurant's decor, took a final sip of coffee and glanced around. 'Right!, we are due to meet here. Half-past.' From an inner pocket of her canvas shoulder bag she held up to a beam of sunlight a small, partially creased colour photograph. 'I'll recognise the eyes for sure, even if he's wearing a veil. Is that him, amongst a group now coming in through the front entrance? No, not him... not the Tuareg in Edmund's photograph, although this was taken quite a few years ago. Wonder if I've got time to pop back to the room for...'

"Madame Stanouton?"

"Oh, er, oui, c'est moi."

"My name is Hamouri. Amadou tells me that you were hoping..."

"Yes… that's right. I'm enormously relieved that you speak English… my French is not what it was once upon a time."

"Amadou said you wished to meet this former work colleague of Monsieur Lanby. Alors, à votre service, Madame!"

"Please call me Elle. Might it be possible for us to find some fresh air, Monsieur Hamouri, it is so stuffy in here. I'm very pleased that we are able to meet… thank you so much for managing to come here this morning."

A biblical raising of be-robed arms opened a narrow pathway through the broadly smiling, colourfully T-shirted 'Donnez-moi stilo, Donnez-moi polaroid' gang – but the manic, conical-hatted Peulh peddling sham Tuareg swords could not be shaken off as the couple made their way across to the bustling *Grand Marché.*

"From here, your famous minaret looks so impressive… as if it has stood there since the beginning of time."

"Tomorrow Elle, if you wish, it is possible to climb to the top."

"That would be very nice, thank you, but what a spectacular market you have. I've never seen sights such as these… except on television of course… but to actually be here! What sounds… smells. How colourfully the women are dressed. Look at these yards upon yards of tie-dyed cloth. Such beautiful batiques. And are these traffic bollards?"

"Ha!, these are pillars of salt from the oases of Fachi and Bilma."

120

"And that crowd over there?"

"People are listening to another tale from Djaram the Storyteller. Listen. Drummers."

"I see them now. Thrilling cross-rhythms. Send shivers down my spine... you Tarzan, me Jane!"

"Qu'est-ce-que-c'est? Viens." Hamouri led his visitor over to the Café Guida.

"Goodness, one can even get ice-cream in Agadez. You know, I'm really looking forward to seeing Ed on Monday..."

"Monday, Elle? Après demain? You go Djanet?"

"Sorry, but who is this person Janet?"

"Djanet... en Algerie... "

Haven't been here 24 hours & already I feel like hi-tailing it home. But have to confess to a misinterpretation of the word Djanet, although it all amounts to the same thing – namely, there wont be any taking up of a room reservation by someone driving up from Lake Chad the day after tomorrow. Hamouri has to be believed i.e. EML telling him he was crossing to Djanet as an alternative route back to UK. Meaning this hotel was told a pack of lies – me too, in that second phone call we had. What a complete waste of my time & money. I positively hate this country all of a sudden. Yet it's Hamouri I feel most sorry for, finding himself stuck with this extremely angry me, until such time as I am capable of deciding when & how best to get back to London.

She flopped on to the double bed, then sat more upright with pillows supporting her shoulders against the wooden headboard, feeling less tense – more relaxed than might otherwise have been the case should she by chance have learned that this same room, this very same bed, had recently been occupied by a certain gentleman from North London. Her handbag with cigarettes and lighter were just beyond reach. The half-closed doors of a tiny wardrobe could not hide the fact that its rail held far more garments than it had originally been her intention to cram into a single suitcase. Her pursed lips became reminded of their ability to smile – just a touch: three pairs of slacks, a second pair of jeans in addition to those being worn, the khaki skirt and bush jacket, numerous tops, and evening attire comprising the chocolate & cream outfit from John Lewis in Oxford Street plus three smart/casual shift dresses. 'And my little black number with heels, stockings, etcetera. Of course. High heels, of course... high hopes more like. More fool me, but then this hotel's nothing like I expected... have ended up bringing ALL the wrong clothes.' She lit up. "Think I'l treat myself to a three-course restaurant lunch, then take to my bed for the rest of the day."

With clicks of the tongue his horse reacts instantly, eager for a dawn canter around the town's perimeter. Hamouri pulls an extra layer of blue cloth tighter around his thin shoulders and stands gazing at the stars. 'Where are you this morning, Eddie... safely across the Ténéré by now, in'shallah.' He reflects on Lanby's secret departure for Djanet oasis with the words ' …if anyone asks, tell them I was seen making for the Zinder Road, which will not be untrue…' Two policemen had paid a call, then nothing more. Until yesterday and that unfortunate moment with *la femme d'Angleterre* – who had requested they meet up again this morning in the hotel lobby.

Madame Stanouton, to his considerable relief, is found to have other issues on her mind; anything other than a certain painful and here-on taboo subject. And they walk whilst they talk, in warm sunshine, an expensive-looking camera in action for the first time, down to *le Vieux Marché.*

"At our meal table last evening the people I flew with from Niamey, two husbands and wives from Neuchâtel in Switzerland… lovely people… told me they'd been refused permission to take an excursion into the mountains."

"Oui Elle, that is because in some regions to the north, even military convoys are being attacked by the rebels. *L' Agence de Voyages* is now without business."

"Meaning certain areas are out of bounds not only to the Swiss, but to this English lady also. Obviously. What a downright shame."

From the old market they stroll back to Café Guida, seating themselves at an outside table with their bottles of Sprite and Pepsi.

"Un moment… Hey, Bazo, ça va? Yes Elle, we see him outside the hotel… he sells my poorer quality items for a small commission. If you are interested, I have in my pocket the very finest Crosses…"

Tuesday 4ᵗʰ February. EML is probably half-way back home by now, but he will not find ME there. Thoroughly enjoying myself. Today, am taking a day off sightseeing, but tomorrow Hamouri has invited me to the house to meet his wife & family. Chance to wear my new (v.old) silver Croix d'In-Gall.

"Lafiya lau" Lanby replied, shaking Adroussa's welcoming hand as he was shown to the newly constructed Rest House. "Tabelot... oui, that's right... HSI sunk wells here and at Telouess around the time of our Kouffaouane contract. I certainly did not expect to see this delightful village again... there might even be others like yourself who remember those Hydro days after what... eight, nine, ten years?" 'Need to recuperate a while', he thought, 'before facing the music. Agadez is only a day's drive from here, but far enough away whilst I try to come up with a convincing account of my whereabouts over the past three weeks. Crucially, my passport shows that I'm still in Niger, legally. It's the Land Rover that'll take some explaining.'

The young *caravaniers* barely recognized the man now dressed in Tuareg clothing and sandals as he pressed monetary notes into their hands. "Laissez-moi ici mes amis... I'll be fine here." Hesitating, Lanby decided not to mention the cargo left behind in the Ténéré, understanding his friends and a local *madugu* named Djibou to be already planning the retrieval of Bilma salt that, with sadness and pride, would be transported the rest of the way to Marandet. "But how can I thank you enough? Merci infiniment, Agaly and Boubaka, for you truly saved my life."

"Madame! Madame!"

"Hamouri… come, please sit down, you are out of breath. Here's some water…"

"Thank you. I'm fine. But you see, two Toyotas from the village near where I was born have just arrived in the market. I know both the drivers and one of them has given me this letter. It is to me and written in English. I ask that you read it, Madame Stanouton."

# FIFTEEN

'When first you set foot on the Dark Continent, my dear, you may tread paths of colonial legacies which many people, to this day even, hold in fond memory.' Mesmerized by the table lamp's late evening blurr of tiny moths and with her thoughts in a whirl, feeling a little awkward that Philip and his sweeping statements should come to mind at this precise moment, she finally put pen to paper:

> Dearest Edmund,
>     Hamouri has shown me your note. Thank God you are safe & well.
>     This brief letter (which he will be taking with him in the morning) is to wish you a swift recovery & hope that before very long we can be together again. I had wanted to deliver this myself, but am told that rebel activities make it inadvisable for me to be a passenger in the convoy up to Tabelot.
> With all my love

Nothing in my life has prepared me for this cartwheeling of emotions, my sheltered suburban life far, far removed from ever contemplating that I might perish from thirst. Eddie's note to Hamouri speaks volumes 'Land Rover crushed by rocks at Adrar Madet, but have been rescued by a camel caravan. I am in Tabelot recovering from the ordeal. Can you get up here? Need your advice regarding my return to Agadez.' I'm finding it almost impossible to imagine what he's endured.

'Cigarette... 'nother drink... can't see myself getting much sleep tonight. Better set the alarm to make sure Hamouri takes my letter. Of utmost concern, is the possibility that some sort of irreparable damage may have been caused.'

Early on this his sixth day at Tabelot, Lanby slung the rucksack over one shoulder and wandered along to his chosen spot beyond the rustling dum palms, where to pass the time reading Arambey's poetry and his own Madet diaries whilst awaiting Hamouri's response to his note; it was widely expected that the Toyotas would be returning from Agadez around midday. But feeling compelled to continue on towards the wadi he made for the trees that lined its bank, acknowledging the cheerful waves of hoe-wielding *jardiniers*. In picking his way through a belt of dense scrub and stepping down on the dry river's edge of loose shale and large stones he realized that he was not alone. "Sannu" he called across to the Targui perched high in the cross-hilted saddle of his fine white camel – to no response as a rhythmic, swaying gait carried them along Oued Telouess towards the Bagzane Massif. Lanby followed, the rider dressed in a light green *chech* and flowing black robes throwing a backward glance, suggesting 'This way – there is something you must see.' ... despite my best efforts in loose gravel, the distance between us remained unchanged. At a bend in the wadi three villagers were stood talking. Arambey – for I now felt certain it was he – raised an arm in salute which, to my concealed anger, they totally ignored. For a good two or three minutes I lost contact. Then, just a few yards away, there stood rider and mount, fully facing me. 'I know', he said, 'that you possessed sufficient belief and this pleased me more than I can say. And I also knew that you would understand my having to leave Madet when I did.' Stunned, I was about to hand him the anthology when his eyes turned to dark shadows. 'You have been a true friend. Read well what is told by the sands. Leave only tracks which others may safely follow. Au revoir, mon ami.' Movement of the veiled lips ceased. Swinging his camel round he rode on, disappearing completely into an all-engulfing dust devil. When viz improved a vortex of clear air whisked the exercise book from my hand, the fierce upcurrent propelling it into a cloudless sky until lost from sight. As I back-tracked, intermittent patches of smooth sand showed only the outline impressions of my sandals – no hoofprints whatsoever of Arambey's camel. So I chucked a rock at a large tree – which passed NOT clean through the middle of something that was not there at all, as half expected, but struck the broad trunk fair and square with a loud thump.

Vehicles! He's here!

Their strategy decided upon and with Hamouri now on his way back down to Agadez to engage in crucial rounds of diplomacy and reasoning, Lanby savoured over and over again Elle's beautiful handwriting and the loving words he thought he'd never live to read. The scribbled copy of his reply, he now realised, had been hasty and somewhat open to misinterpretation.

Then at around the time he imagined Hamouri being successful, or otherwise, in his securing from Inspector Maïga an absolving *laissez-passer*, he took a metaphoric look over his shoulder in seeking to draw a line under it all. To, if not soon arrested for his transgressions, pick up from where he left off: where they left off.

128

The desert calls   Has to be answered   Changing one's
life forever   Adieu then   Never will I forget your silence
Above all your Providence   Be not too serious   And
listen well to the wind in the Acacia trees   As in desert
sands   One leaves tracks that...

At which point Lanby slid pen and notebook into the rucksack
and made his way back down to the wadi.

# SIXTEEN

In mid-morning sunshine *le Grand Marché* was a-buzz with rumours that France had been asked to mediate a truce between the Niger Government and the resurgent *Front de Liberation de l'Aïr et de l'Azzaouad*, the atmosphere still tense a week after Tuareg rebels had attacked a military patrol south of Arlit with the dead reported to number between eighty and one hundred. Awaiting the arrival time, Hamouri found himself urged by some of his contemporaries to again describe his meeting at *le Commissariat* and how he'd managed to negotiate the Englishman's safe passage down from Tabelot, no charges brought or further questions asked. There'd come the painful task of breaking the tragic news to Bazo – and now his good friends were preparing to return home. Tomorrow evening, Tinna would prepare the farewell meal.

"What's the time?" Her enquiry was aimed at checking whether or not the third-hand watch bought the day before yesterday still worked. "Twenty past", he replied, "Said we'd meet up at half-ten." For once free from any pestering they stepped out into the warm air, again having missed breakfast, and for a leg stretch chose the circuitous route. 'Just love this place' she wrestled with her thoughts, 'so why, in fact do we really HAVE to leave in the next two or three days, depending on Hamouri's update re getting to Niamey by road or air? No, we don't, but I still cannot summon up the courage to…

and also ask what's the sense in hurrying back to London in the middle of a freezing cold February.' Before over-sleeping, Eleanor had in the early hours lain wide awake wondering how best to put her case without Mitch – the name she was thrilled to be using again – without Mitch killing her proposal stone dead.

The days following his arrival from Tabelot had seen her observing his every move, listening intently to his every word in case, just in case there came a tell-tale sign that things, for whatever reason, were not as they should be following such an ordeal – not as she'd known them to be prior to last December. Yet all seemed fine. Thus far. Now, however, there was this test of her endurance at evening meal-times – his beer-charged monologues during which she found it hard to venture even half-meaningful view-points, for or against, when faced with yet another sand dune sermon. So instead she'd come to nodding in the right places whilst pondering the answers to a 9 Across or a 12 Down; no clues ever touching Solo Circumnavigation, Planetary Distances or Powerful Presence. But wonderful were the nights cuddled up in a double bed with the man she truly understood, living in the present, vibrantly alive to this opportunity they had to give their relationship another try.

'You know what, Elle', she unmercifully teased herself as they approached the market, 'if you were to be brutally honest with yourself, the real reason you don't wish to go home yet-awhiles is because it has become impossible for you to commence each morning without first sitting up in bed, yanking the spare pillow behind your back and listening to the unrestrained laughter of people scurrying past the shuttered window on their way to market. And stroking his naked shoulder, contemplating the garments you'd carefully chosen which, after nightcaps, he had chivalrously removed then just thrown over the chair.'

To her hidden delight, Hamouri explained that FLAA activities had forced Air Niger to withhold all further announcements regarding flights to Niamey.

"It's possible to go by road, though, isn't it?"

"Yes Eddie, minibuses are still making that journey."

They continued their stroll between lines of whirring sewing machines. This morning there were just two fly-blown meat stalls. As they reached a small group stood listening to another tale from the blind Targui she knew that if she did not say what had been on her mind for the past four days then she may as well remain eternally silent – for not in a one-to-one but now surrounded by people the timing could be perfect.

Elle squeezed Mitch's hand. "You won't believe this darling, but Aunt Daphne, rest in peace, remembered me in her Will... a lot of money... I've been left a lot of money, which means that we can afford to prolong our stay here, should we wish. Checked with reception who say that will be fine. What do you think?"

"You're joking!"

"Look darling, I know how very much you are looking forward to getting back... I won't be so presumptuous as to say that I understand how deep this need might now be to return to UK, to civilization and all that, after what you've been through, but..."

"Elle, beautiful Elle, are you seriously suggesting that we stay on in that cramped room for what, another week or two?"

"Just a month… not stuck in the hotel but hiring a vehicle, which we can now well afford. Drive south, where it is not yet forbidden to travel… I do so very much wish to see more of this country. Just you and I. See the Sahara. Together!"

Lanby sought the space needed to consider so totally unacceptable and absurd an idea by edging forwards slightly, peering over shoulders whilst muttering a rhetorical "Did you hear that, Hamouri?" 'Clearly she's given this a great deal of thought. Why bring the subject up now? This is what you find… Not! We can discuss it tonight.' Her right hand re-engaged his left. Gesturing with pursed lips Hamouri whispered "The old man is telling the story of the Tree again." 'Yes, Mr Fixit, I'm sure you would also see Elle's suggestion as ludicrous… out of the question… and in your very polite way you would probably say that having recently been rescued from the desert Monsieur Eddie may not care if he doesn't see another camel, ever again, and driving across the desert he's had up to here!' Suddenly conscious that his right hand had shot up to beneath his chin he pretended that he was on the point of saying something.

"Yes Mitch?"

"Er… there's no likelyhood of this happening , of course… but just for the sake of argument, which area south from here can one honestly describe as worthy of a visit?"


"Lake Chad, darling."

Staring straight ahead, Lanby resignedly waited for the unseeing, milky-blue eyes to meet his – a sealing of fate once again by the veiled smile of Djaram the Storyteller.

With a burning thirst the creature of open desert pauses to sniff the air. Warily it approaches the foot of the mountain, muzzles caps that will not open then thrusts its nose into a shallow pool of water. As a second blue plastic bowl is licked dry the old bull Addax senses danger and hurridly retreats towards a line of dunes.

A mile from Adrar Madet the lead vehicle brakes hard in a cloud of dust. A pair of similarly camouflaged cab-truck Toyotas draw alongside, their open backs filled with soldiers, rifles between knees. Climbing on to the bonnet a youthful *Lieutenant* trains his binoculars on the source of reflected sunlight. He orders his men to load their weapons. Radio contact is re-established with Dirkou Fort. A three-pronged attack will cut off the rebels' escape route, but as they bear down on the Land Rover a 'Hold your fire' is called.

*Les militaries* light cigarettes and wander around, forbidden to touch a single thing, exchanging comments about the crushed vehicle and the neat lines of jerrycans. Most wear sunglasses in preference to their army issue goggles. One carries an enormous transistor radio over his shoulder.

As the officer and his second in command earnestly discuss the message, the abandoned tent and the direction arrow fashioned from rocks, there come shouts of "Amillal... Biche ..." Rifle barrels point to fresh tracks – splayed hoof tracks of an Addax antelope that cannot be far away. For those expecting the order to give chase a fire is already lit. Fresh meat. *Mechoui.*

Another distorted exchange with Dirkou: '... proceed immediately to L'Arbre, then return to base, as instructed.'